To My Dear Slimeball

RICH MILLER

HARVEST HOUSE PUBLISHERS
Eugene, Oregon 97402

Except where otherwise indicated, all Scripture quotations in this book are taken from the New American Standard Bible, © 1960, 1962, 1963, 1968, 1971, 1972, 1973, 1975, 1977 by The Lockman Foundation. Used by permission.

Verses marked NIV are taken from the Holy Bible, New International Version®. Copyright © 1973, 1978, 1984 by the International Bible Society. Used by permission of Zondervan Publishing House. The "NIV" and "New International Version" trademarks are registered in the United States Patent and Trademark Office by International Bible Society.

TO MY DEAR SLIMEBALL

Copyright ©1995 by Harvest House Publishers
Eugene, Oregon 97402

Library of Congress Cataloging-in-Publication Data

Miller, Rich, 1954–
   To my dear Slimeball / Rich Miller.
      p.   cm.
   Summary: In a series of memos, a high-level demon instructs his apprentice
in methods of luring a teenage boy to succumb to Satan.
   ISBN 1-56507-187-5
   [1. Demonology--Fiction. 2. Conduct of life--Fiction. 3. Christian life--
Fiction.] I. Title.
PZ7.M63333To   1995
[Fic]--dc20   94-46957
                                                                  CIP
                                                                  AC

All rights reserved. No portion of this book may be reproduced in any form without the written permission of the Publisher.

Printed in the United States of America.

95 96 97 98 99 00 01 02 / 10 9 8 7 6 5 4 3 2 1

To my conquering hero,
the Lord Jesus Christ—
who won the war so that
we can win the battles

Foreword

I was raised in a religious home that taught me to believe in God and required me to attend church. I did both voluntarily and tried to live a moral life, believing that I would go to heaven if I did.

Then I encountered God. I entered into an incredible new life. I was spiritually alive, and my eyes were opened to the truth of God's Word. I realized that I had been playing church, and only giving lip service to the reality of God and the spiritual world.

The apostle John says, "The whole world lies in the power of the evil one" (1 John 5:19). The apostle Paul says, "Our struggle is not against flesh and blood, but against the rulers, against the powers, against the world forces of this darkness, against the spiritual forces of wickedness . . ." (Ephesians 6:12).

Satan is a defeated foe, and yet he "prowls about like a roaring lion, seeking someone to devour" (1 Peter 5:8). He accomplishes this primarily through deception: "He is a liar, and the father of lies" (John 8:44); he "has blinded the minds of the unbelieving" (2 Corinthians 4:4); and he preys on the minds of believers. That is why Paul says, "I am afraid, lest as the serpent deceived Eve by his craftiness, your minds should be led astray from the simplicity

5

and purity of devotion to Christ" (2 Corinthians 11:3).

Paul also says, "The Spirit explicitly says that in later times some will fall away from the faith, paying attention to deceitful spirits and doctrines of demons" (1 Timothy 4:1). We at Freedom in Christ Ministries have discovered that this battle for the mind is going on all over the world. Praise God we have an answer in Christ, and His truth will set us free (John 8:32).

And praise God for Rich Miller, who directs our Freedom in Christ Youth Ministry in the Eastern United States. He not only understands this battle, he knows how to help people find their freedom in Christ. Rich has spoken to thousands of students around the world. He understands youth culture and the struggles young people are having.

To My Dear Slimeball is more than a literary novel inspired by C.S. Lewis' *The Screwtape Letters*. Rich has given us a fresh glimpse of the battle going on in the spiritual realm, which threatens to destroy our families and bring tragic defeat to the youth of the world. This book will open people's eyes to Satan's schemes, caution them to fix their eyes on Jesus, the author and perfecter of faith (Hebrews 12:2), and admonish them to take every thought captive in obedience to Christ (2 Corinthians 10:5).

The devil can't make us do anything, but he will try to deceive us, falsely accuse us, and tempt us to live our lives independent of God. We must assume the responsibility to establish our identity and find our freedom in Christ. Our assignment is to recognize the lie, choose the truth, and win the battle for our minds. May the grace of God enable you to do just that.

Dr. Neil T. Anderson,
President, Freedom in Christ Ministries

Introduction

The Bible tells us that God loves us and that He is at work in our lives to cleanse us from sin and draw us close to His heart. To accomplish this, He has already made the ultimate Fatherly sacrifice in sending His Son, the Lord Jesus Christ to live, die, and live again. That was God's incredible plan from the beginning—to bring us home again through Jesus.

But there is one who stands in direct opposition to the plan of God. His name is Satan—the devil. He is the tempter (Matthew 4:3), the deceiver (Revelation 13:14), and the source of all lies (John 8:44). He delights in accusing God's people, constantly trying to convince them that they are worthless, powerless, guilty sinners.

The Word of God, however, declares the people of God to be saints, holy ones, dearly loved by God, and freed from sin (Philippians 1:1, Colossians 3:12, Revelation 1:5).

Clearly there is a major battle going on for the souls of people, and the battleground is the *mind*. It is a war between truth and lies, between God's revelation and Satan's deception.

Jesus loves us and wants to set us free from *all* bondage. The devil hates us and is committed to trying to spiritually drug us and drag us away from God. Sometimes we feel like there's a gigantic cosmic tug-of-war going on between good and evil—and we're the rope!

The great news is that the war is over. Jesus Christ came for the very purpose of destroying the works of the devil (1 John 3:8), and He succeeded!

The question is not whether Jesus will win the war. That's already been decided. The question is whether God's people, believers in Christ, will win those daily battles against our archenemy, the devil.

What is the key to daily victory? The truth. We must *know* the truth, *believe* the truth, and *choose to live out* the truth in the power of the Spirit of truth—the Holy Spirit. It is the truth that sets us free (John 8:32).

Sometimes a good way to understand something is to see it in contrast to its opposite. For example, the color white looks brightest when placed next to the color black. A cold shower feels even colder when you've just come out of a sauna.

That's what this book is meant to do: to make the truth of God stand out in sharp contrast to the lies and deceptions of Satan. This story exposes the wiles and tactics of our enemy, the devil, so that our eyes and hearts can be opened to the truth.

The book opens with a letter of introduction from the demon, Spitwad, to his master-demon, Slimeball. Spitwad has just entered the United States after a "tour of duty" in Thailand. He wants to make a good first impression—but fails miserably.

The rest of the story consists of reports and instructions from that high-level demon, Slimeball, to his new apprentice, Spitwad. When Slimeball writes, imagine you are looking at the negatives of a roll of film. Slimeball's way of looking at things is the *exact opposite* of God's way. What Slimeball hates, God (whom Slimeball refers to as "the Adversary" or "the Light") loves. What Slimeball wants to tempt us to do, God wants us to stay away from. You'll get the picture as you read on.

Now, I don't happen to believe that demons actually talk to one another by means of letters. Their communication network is much more sophisticated than that.

Nor do I believe their language is as clean as you will find here. I have toned down Slimeball's language a lot. Nobody would publish this book if I used the profanity that demons actually use!

The story centers on a fairly typical high school student named David. Spitwad is assigned to be his "guardian demon" and he has the job of doing everything in his power to help mess up David's life. Actually David does a pretty good job of that on his own!

There are a lot of twists and turns in the plot and things look pretty dark for a while. This is no candy-coated, syrupy story, but then again, neither is real life.

While you're enjoying the book, may God grant you, through this unusual approach, a brighter, full-color picture of the truth.

And maybe, if you're honest with yourself, you

may come to see how the devil has succeeded in spiritually drugging and dragging *you* away from the God who loves you. It's kind of like finally waking up from a bad dream that seemed to last forever. Or like moping around on a dreary, foggy, drizzly day when all of a sudden the sun breaks through the clouds. That's often the way God works.

If you are already one of God's kids, a child of the Light, this book will provide the ammo you need to stand strong against the darkness that seeks to silently creep into every life.

In the back of the book you'll find *Steps to Freedom in Christ.* I encourage you to work through this section. Better yet, have your youth pastor or leader guide you through it.

Do you want to be free from the pain of the past, problems of the present, and fears of the future? The *Steps to Freedom in Christ* is a great tool to help you out of bondage and into the freedom of God's Spirit.

For now, sit back and relax as we eavesdrop on a rather secret and sinister conversation outside a typical suburban home.

To my dear Slimeball,

I can't believe I'm actually in the United States! This is like a nightmare come true for me; I am so excited! Me and Droolcup made it through the Hellis Island Demon Immigration and Ugliness Station (HIDIUS) two days ago, and they told me that you would be my mentor. Do you realize how lucky you are?

Just so you're not my tormentor! Get it? Ha ha! Pretty funny, right?

In case you have never heard of me, my name is Spitwad, and I've spent the last 100 years or so in Thailand. Hey, listen to this: Your name is Slimeball and mine is Spitwad. Isn't that cool? It's like I'm a part of you or something. Don't you get it? Spit is kind of like a part of slime, you know. And a wad is like a small ball! I guess you could say I'm a little spit off the old slime, eh Slimer?

You and me are gonna work great together. I've got the brains and you've got the well . . . age. Together we'll be unbeatable. I can't wait to get to work. What are we going to start with, a house-haunting? Or maybe a little spiritual channeling action? Hey, that would be great. I hear those guys make really good money. And the fame. Wow! Maybe I could call myself Zandor—or something like that. I could speak through some glassy-eyed idiot and tell everyone I'm a ten-million-year-old space traveler who's come to earth to help save it from the environmentalists!

Ha ha! Just a little bit of politically incorrect humor there, ol' Slumbucket. You're not one of those snooty, self-important, always-pulling-rank kind of demons, are you? I sure hope not. But hey, with a name like Slimeball, how could you be?

Yeah, I can see it now. We're going to get along just great. I'm sure you're laughing your head off as you read this—you are, aren't you?

Hey, I've got to tell you that me and Droolcup decided to buzz over to a pro football game yesterday. That was awesome! Over 80,000 screaming fans going crazy over 22 guys on the field trying to move around a piece of leather. Unbelievable!

But here's the really cool part. Before the game we decided to drop in on a local church's worship service, where a few of those 80,000 fans attend, to see what mischief we could raise. It was amazing! The people were dead quiet, except for the hymn singing, of course. They didn't seem very interested in the pastor's teaching from the Bible—even though it was covered with leather, too! We didn't need to do much there.

I think I'm really going to like it here in the good ol' USA. These Americans really seem to have their priorities aligned with ours.

Hey, Scumbreath, have you heard this one? How many demons does it take to change a light bulb? Give up? Two. One to unscrew the good bulb and the other to find a burned out one to replace it! Ha ha. Pretty good, huh? I made that one up myself.

Since we're going to be working so closely, I guess I should lay it all on the line right from the start. I don't work during "Bewitched" reruns. You don't know how hard it was all those years in the jungles of Thailand without TV. Pretty gruesome! Also, if I happen to be absorbed in the latest Stephen King novel, I will not answer my beeper.

I heard this vicious rumor when I was passing through HIDIUS (and say it ain't so, Slimer ol' pal) that I might be working with a *teenager*. You know—one of those young humans. Oooh, even the sound of the word gives me the creeps.

I mean, I didn't work with teenagers in the jungles of Thailand! What would I do with one? Would I have to stay until he grows up? Ugh!

But on the other hand, it seems like some people make a career out of never quite growing up. Maybe he's one of those. Hmm. On second thought, maybe that ain't so bad after all. I could get into that actually. Hanging out in the video arcade at the mall all day, watching the tube all night. Okay, I think I can handle it. Bring on the teenage toxic waste 'cause I'm ready!

So cheer down, ol' Oozeorb, 'cause Spitwad's here. Aw c'mon, wipe that smile off your face. Remember: Every silver lining has a cloud. It'll be sheer pan*demoni*um, just you wait and see.

I'm waiting to hear from you.

Your most worthy student,

Spitwad

The one who dies with the most toys ... loses!

I received your "letter of introduction" today and could barely contain myself while reading it. You are without a doubt the most impudent, bratty, insolent, disrespectful and messed-up spirit I've ever had the displeasure of knowing!

And oh, don't worry. I've heard of you before all right. Every other joke down here is about you. Have you heard this one? How many Spitwads does it take to change a light bulb? Give up? I'll spare you the boring details.

Now, "Slumbucket," "Scumbreath," and "Oozeorb" were obnoxious enough. But "Slimer ol' pal" takes the cake. Don't even think about becoming "buddy, buddy" with me, you piece of cosmic dung.

Don't you realize, Mucusmound, whom you are addressing? *I* am Slimeball Y. Boonswoggle, deceiver extraordinaire, perfect prefect of the principality in which you now reside.

Unfortunately, I have had the dreary job of following your miserable career until now. Your recent tour of duty in Thailand was enough to make even one so tough and rugged as myself sick to my stomach. No doubt you and your buddy Droolcup are giving each other high-five's at your recent *promotion*. Promotion, ha! You can just stop patting each other on the back. You were moved from tempting tribal people in Thailand to teenagers in America because I have been commanded to keep a closer watch on you.

I'm sure your feeble mind is wondering why. I'll tell you *why*. It's because you are simply the biggest nerd in all our Father Satan's kingdom. That's why!

If I had *my* way, I would have sent you directly from Thailand to Fryland. You know, "h-e-double toothpicks." However, Our Most Worthy Master, cunning and clever as he is, has ordered you to the United States. He feels that your experience with those who dabble in witchcraft should be of some service here—especially in this time which fools call the "New" Age.

Anyway, any experience you can gain while working with American high school students could greatly help our cause when you are shipped off again (very soon, I hope!) to the ends of the earth.

You must realize one big difference between Asia and America, my slave. In Asia you worked out in the open and people feared you (thank the devil they never actually *saw* you!). In America, you will work in secret and people will not even believe you are there! That is how far advanced this country has become.

We laugh at their pride. They think they have the world by the tail with all their science and technology. Soon they will know that the tail is attached to a dragon who will one day eat them alive!

Now, in answer to your first question: No, you idiot! That is not a spirit house in the front yard of your new home in the suburbs. And I am not at all interested in how quickly you made the bird that was nesting in there fly away.

Go *inside* the big house, you jerk. That's where the people live. There are plenty of electronic boxes in their home in which you can live for now.

Your host is a 15-year-old white male from an upper-middle class family. Make note of this: Much of his already fast-disappearing time and energy will be spent keeping up with what is "in." It doesn't really matter what it is—the latest music video, a mindless sitcom on TV, a late-night show, computer or video games, movies, clothing, etc. Use anything as long as it is hip, flip and fast-moving.

By the way, an important principle to keep in mind is that most Americans never really grow out of this way of life. They always get excited about what is state of the art or the latest fashion or craze.

Their toys simply become more expensive the older they get. I've known countless humans we've led around on a never-ending search for satisfaction—from car, vacation, house, home entertainment system, boat, jewelry, and on and on—until the day they drop dead.

What fun it is to watch them delight in their new pride and joy only to have us quickly turn their eyes to something even "better." The trick is to keep them thinking that the next "it" will finally make them happy and satisfied.

19

Our job is to *gratify* their passions. The Adversary's job is to *satisfy* their souls' deepest longings. As long as you do your job well, your host will never know what he's missed. That is really quite easy to do. If it's faster, flashier or has the latest features, he'll go for it like a hungry trout after fresh bait.

Anyway, each new object of his lust and greed simply becomes a new link in the chain that will bind your host closer to your heart. Oh, how touching! You would do well to start attaching this chain around your young host right away.

Make sure he takes smug satisfaction in being able to talk about and own what is "new and in." His friends at school will think he's cool. That is the ultimate ego trip for the American teenager.

Of course, he'll never even notice that the only thing really *cool* about him will be his heart as we slowly freeze it. Even better for us if he learns to cleverly put other people down who are not "in." Intimidation is a way he can achieve control over those around him—something he wants very badly.

And once he gains control of others, he will be worshiped because he will be feared. That is what he *really* wants. And so do we.

Of course, I shouldn't need to remind you (but I will anyway, knowing how thick-headed you are!) to keep the religion of the Risen One as something old, confusing and boring to your host. If you do that, you can expect your relationship together to be a long and fruitful one.

More on the subject of boredom later. I actually have great hopes for you in that area. You have shown a tremendous ability for boring me already!

Your superior,

Slimeball

Leaven is rolling
in the dough

To most worthless Spitwad,

Now that you are settled into your new home and have gotten acquainted with your new host a bit, it is time to let you in on our little secret. This is maximum security stuff, you understand, and is in no way ever to be leaked to any mortal. Is that crystal clear? If you fail in this matter, you will not fail again. I guarantee it. I even suggest that you forget that I ever sent this letter to you. You will see why quite soon.

All is not as peaceful as it may seem in sleepy, little Suburbia, USA, where you live. If George Washington knew what was going on in "the land of the free and the home of the brave" he would roll over in his grave.

They call themselves simply *Leaven*. And that is what they are—agents of change. Like yeast that works its way through a lump of dough to make it rise, they are trying to infiltrate all power centers of society—local, state and national levels—to gradually influence society to come to *our* standards. They are already well on their way.

The people belonging to your local coven live and work in your town or in the city. In fact, they *are* the city. Even though official Leaven members are a very select group, their network of influence is vast. For them, money is no object and wealth is simply a ticket to power and pleasure. In reality, to them, power *is* pleasure. It is what they lust for, live for, and long for. To them, life is power and power is life. I couldn't agree with them more.

Our instructions regarding Leaven and their activities are simple, Splitworm, "Hands off!" The agent in charge is about as close to our Most Strategic Master as anyone can get (or would *want* to get, I might add!).

I saw him once, I think. He was like a shadow at twilight or the chill in the air when a cloud swiftly crosses the sun. He is a faint movement caught out of the corner of one's eye and gone before you can turn your head to look. He is known only by his code name, Eclipse.

He was one of the first to defect over to our Master's side in the Great Rebellion. His thirst for power cannot be quenched—like a black hole in space can't be filled. He is cunning and vicious, seeking to absorb all matter and energy into himself.

Leaven members worship him and he seems to tolerate them. They stupidly think they have some control over him. Does the mouse control the cat? Eclipse will use them until they no longer serve his purpose. Then he will dissolve them.

Eclipse is obsessed with destroying every last glimmer of the Light. He is far more than a common tempter, and much more than a brilliant deceiver. He is a cold, calculating, cruel killer. An assassin. He is terror by night—the plague that stalks in the darkness.

So far as I am concerned (which isn't very far), "Hands off!" is sound advice for all of us!

Leaven and Eclipse have their agenda and we have ours. Leaven pulls the strings in society's arenas of power—government, media, business, education, military, medicine, law, sports and entertainment.

You name it, they're there. And Eclipse pulls Leaven's strings. The puppeteer pulls the big puppets' strings and the big puppet pulls the strings of the little puppets. A nice arrangement, don't you think?

What kind of lies does Eclipse feed the hungry Leavenites? The full New Age meal-plan (including the standard bill-of-fare): "You achieve what you believe," "You create your own reality because you are god," "Jesus is an Ascended Master, an avatar who taught reincarnation," and "All is God and God is all and all is one." You know, the standard New Age party line.

They swallow it all. Why? Because Leaven members are first and foremost in love with themselves, and the rest of the world can jump off a cliff!

They live by the Golden Rules: "He who has the gold, rules!" "Do unto others before they have a chance to do unto you." All that good stuff. They actually despise each other, based on their obsessive fear that someone else may become more powerful than them!

That's why they have all their rules and checks and balances. And that's one reason they have their meetings—to keep an eye on each other. They also hold their sacrifices—it gives them a power "fix"—and plan their strategies. But the thing they do best is control each other. It's kind of like Spy vs. Spy vs. Spy vs. Spy vs. Spy . . .

The question, "Is it right?" has little or no meaning to Leaven. The burning question for them is, "Does it work?"

So why the direct link-up with Eclipse? Why did they buy into the hard-core Satanism stuff? They were looking for an edge, something that would propel them light years ahead of the common, garden-variety, New Age incense sniffer.

Besides, who wants to mess around with crystals when you can have diamonds? Who cares about levitating a book when you can control the rise and fall of a nation? Why play around with Tarot cards and tea leaves to try and predict the future when you can *make* the future?

And Eclipse provides a rather nice, all-inclusive package of power, prosperity and prestige for "our" people. Eclipse is their edge. And that's why they'll do whatever he tells them to do.

So what does all this Leaven stuff have to do with you? Well, if you ask me, Eclipse would do well to steer as clear of your bungling as he possibly can. But, somehow, I think you will become tangled up in this whole bloody mess. Why do I say that? Because your host's busy, gone-most-of-the-time father just happens to hold a very important job. Where? At a certain major corporation that manufactures and sells jet fighters to the government.

So what's the point? Leaven controls its board of directors. A little Leaven changes the whole corporation.

Your superior spy,

Slimeball

Lighthouses in Suburbia, USA

To most worthless Spitwad,

Now I know you are very curious about what Leaven is up to these days. To be honest (which is usually such a waste of time), so am I. But orders are orders. Remember that curiosity killed the kitty, as they say. And, I dare say that your reasons for being curious are far more immature than mine.

I am deeply concerned that Eclipse and the gang are going to try something really stupid that will botch up all *my* years of hard labor in this principality.

You, on the other hand, are curious only because you hope to be involved somehow in what Leaven is up to. Have you been watching those *Omen* movies again? How many times do I have to tell you that no news about Leaven is good news!

Now, it's time we get down and dirty with the business of tempting and tormenting your teenage twerp.

You seemed upset when you found out that your host attends church with his family on Sundays. You've noticed, of course, that daddy dear doesn't go. He says he can worship better on the golf course. In one way he's right, you know. When he rides around in his golf cart, slamming that little white ball into the trees, sand and water, he uses our Adversary's name more than some ministers! That kind of worship we'll encourage any day.

Your host's father should be a great help to you, by the way. Make sure the brat listens well when dear ol' dad passes on the messages we whisper in his ear like, "Religion is for little kids and old ladies, son. A real man depends on himself." Or, "I think it's good to attend church regularly. That's what *I* do. I go every Christmas and Easter!"

Anyway, back to the subject of "lighthouses," or churches as the humans call them. Your host has been dragged off to the First Dead Church of Suburbia (or whatever it is called) since he was a screaming, little baby. He is clueless as to what a true Christian is. And as long as he snoozily slurps up Pastor Bilgewater's sleepy sermons every Sunday, he will stay in that spiritually drugged state.

Keep your eyes on the leering lad as he practically drools over the blond-haired floozy who always sits in the pew in front of him. The way she dresses gives the teenage lust-bucket's eyes plenty of fuel for his frothy fantasies. If nothing else works, she should keep him coming back for another religious "hit" every Sunday.

Bilgewater is a rather sorry excuse for a minister, but so much the better for us. Leaven actually owns him, though he has no clue they even exist. He would be powerless to do anything, even if he did know. Our "yeast" brethren have puppets who control his church council. Other Leavenites actually hold the reins of the entire denomination and its seminaries.

Believe me, Bilgewater is on a leash, and should he ever start pulling and straining against it, he will simply hang himself on the choke collar that Leaven put on him.

That minister knows less about the Light than we do! (Oh, how I wish we did not know so much. I am still haunted by the horrible memory of that scorching, blistering brightness of the Son as He blazed fire from His eyes and sent us reeling from our home in heaven to this desert wasteland called earth! I shudder every time something reminds me of that day. We must try hard not to think about it—and the judgment that hangs over each of our heads like a time bomb waiting to go off.)

Back to Bilgewater. He has mentally ripped out all the verses in his Bible that cannot be scientifically proven to actually be the words of Jesus. He was a big fan of that "scholarly seminar" where they tried to decide what Jesus had *really* said. About all he's left with are "the Golden Rule" and a few verses on giving money.

But he considers himself to be a "well-read man"—a quality he constantly reminds the congregation of as he quotes from many of *our* favorite poets and philosophers.

I warn you, Spitwad, be on the alert at all times! There's always a Bible-reading in their church service, more out of tradition than anything else. Don't be a fool! Don't ever forget what even one sentence of that cursed Book can do! Every bit of it is dangerous when the Adversary pulls His sword from His belt and starts swinging it at our throats! It sings with a dreadful, ear-piercing power that can slash to shreds years of our work in an instant! I have wounds that still sting . . . but not too much, of course.

There are other churches like Bilgewater's in town, but you need not concern yourself with them. The one to watch is the Lighthouse at Fifth and Elm. They say that they want to live and love the way the first churches did. This is extremely dangerous. They give every indication of being very serious about staying connected to their King.

Some of your host's friends from the football team go to this church. They have a very active youth group which is well-known and fairly well respected at the school. They have brought in pro athletes to speak and hold well-attended Christian concerts for youth. Those friends of your host have been inviting him to come to youth group on Sunday nights. In fact, one of his closest friends, a boy named Steve, is of particular concern. I tell you, Spitwad, there is great danger there!

Fortunately, your host's parents view the people in that church as religious fanatics and Jesus freaks. This will help some, but peer pressure is a powerful force for both evil and good in a teenager's life. Never forget that, Spinewimp.

I do have some good news, however. Our friends from Leaven have managed to infiltrate the football team as well. One day we may need to avail ourselves of Eclipse's services.

Another advantage we have is that, like a lot of 15-year-olds, your host has a lazy, procrastination streak in him. "Why do today what I can put off until tomorrow?" is his motto. That's very helpful to us. Distract him as much as you can during the weekend so that he neglects to do his homework until Sunday dinnertime. Then he will *have* to stay home Sunday nights instead of going to the Lighthouse youth group. His parents will see to that.

That's what I like about so many "Christian" homes. When a kid gets too busy or undisciplined in his life, the first thing to go is any "excess" spiritual stuff.

If it turns out that he has no homework, simply encourage him to flip through the 72 channels of his electronic mind pulverizer (alias TV set). He'll find something to keep his brain (and I use the term loosely) occupied.

By the way, have you ever seen any of the *Friday the 13th* or *Nightmare on Elm Street* movies? Fine family entertainment. You can shiver with the purest glee as you watch your host's ten-year-old brother devour those kinds of films. He actually *loves* being scared to death! We'll gladly give the young fool all the fear he can handle . . . and much more. Ah, what delight to plant seeds of terror in such young, tender soil!

Before I close, I need to make you aware of one more large church in town. They have done much serious harm to us in the past, especially in their terrible devotion to preaching that hated gospel. There still remains a fairly impressive army of saints there.

Most of them, however, feel very uncomfortable about what is going on over at the Fifth and Elm Lighthouse. This is to our advantage. If we can't keep churches from preaching the gospel, at least we can keep them isolated from one another.

If they knew the power they had in uniting in love and prayer against us. . . . We should thank our Most Deceptive Father daily that this remains one of the hardest things for churches to do . . . to actually love each other! It is an absolute delight to see them squabble and quarrel and storm off in a huff from each other because they don't agree on some minor point of doctrine. What perfect glee it is to watch churches split over such trivial pursuits as: "Should we have pews or chairs in the sanctuary?"

They are so blind that they do not see that their true unity is not based on believing all the same things, but in having the same Lord! They are all part of the same family, brothers and sisters in Christ. We continue to hold sway in this community because they keep acting like most brothers and sisters. They fight!

One final note, Spitwad, and your concrete skull must somehow find a way to absorb this: Your host's grandmother (his mother's mother, that is) is one of the genuine saints in that conservative church's army. She has been in the Light ever since HeartFreezer (may he melt in torment!) let her get away from him 62 years ago. And she prays. Oh, the stinking, puking smell of those prayers . . . like the cheapest incense! I hate it!!

But mark my words, Spittoon, the Adversary loves it. And He listens to her.

She is praying for your host and his family. Our efforts to stop her mindless devotion to prayer have so far failed. I repeat, *so far*. We have attacked her with pain, illness, ridicule, rejection from her family, loneliness and discouragement. But the One to whom she prays unfairly surrounds her with the meanest herd of angelic goons you'd ever want—uh, *not want* to see! And so she keeps on praying, like a maddening mosquito humming in our ears.

Take note and note it well, Spitwad. Somewhere along the line our Adversary is going to make a strong move for your host's soul, in response to this woman's prayers. You must be ready to launch an immediate counterattack. I have warned you in advance.

Still your superior,

Slimeball

33

Busyness is next to ungodliness

To most worthless Spitwad,

Do you remember the old saying, "Idle hands are the devil's workshop?" That half-truth was popular during your host's parents' childhood days. That proverb was actually one of our scare tactics, and an extremely clever one, by our Most Wise and Wicked Master. He roared that half-truth at the poor humans, sending them running scared from the evils of laziness. But they failed to see our glistening teeth and drooling mouths eager to greet them at the other extreme: the rat race of busyness.

By the way, my young apprentice, I trust you remember your Deception 101 class? Professor Twilight tried to drill into your swelled head the value of mixing a little truth with a little lie. That's far more effective than direct lying, at least at first. Once we have the human rats nibbling on the tasty cheese of half-truth, they will eventually want to chomp down on the whole chunk. They'll feel so content that they'll never even notice the poisonous lies we've hidden inside. They'll swallow the whole thing, and then it will be too late for them.

But back to the business of busyness. It used to be,

in the old days, that Sunday was a day for church and rest. Some Light-lovers would even consider the day a time for getting close to God again. What a horrible waste of time, if you ask me!

Well, if you hadn't already noticed (and knowing you, you probably *hadn't* noticed), things have changed. More stores are open on Sundays, sporting events take place without a second thought, and life is not much different than the other six days of the week. Ah, progress.

Your host's family proudly marches out of Bilgewater's church every Sunday, a silent "Amen" on their lips. Translation: "Boy am I glad this is over for another week!"

Their "Christian duty" complete, having paid their dues in the country-club offering plate, they give a sigh of relief and prepare to *really* enjoy the rest of the day.

Watch the mad flurry of activity that explodes into action once they burst in the door at home. Mother, after jamming some processed food down their greedy gullets, will shuttle one brat off to a soccer game and another one to gymnastics practice. Ah, such rest!

Your host himself will be off and running with his pack of friends to the true place of American Sunday worship—the local mall! There you can witness, Spitwad, the real "in God we trust" of these materialistic-mad humans.

Did they have trouble finding a parking spot at church? Not likely. But just try and find one at the mall!!

I especially love your host's famous magic act. Dollars which mysteriously disappeared when the offering plate went by, will wondrously reappear from your host's pocket the moment he sets foot in the video arcade.

This is all very good for our business, and is to be encouraged as much as possible. Not just on Sundays, mind you, but every day. Our goal is for everyone to be so active that they are on the brink of exhaustion most of the time. Then our friends disease, stress, anger, impatience and cruel words can have a field day!

This whole busyness/weariness cycle is considered pretty normal nowadays in most families. In fact, if you can believe this, many people pride themselves on how busy and tired they are! As if that was the way their Creator wanted them to be all the time! We know better, but will we tell?

Just watch your host's mother (or is she his private chauffeur?) when she writes the yearly yawner known as the Xmas family newsletter. (By the way, it is only right that we call Christmas *Xmas* anyway. Since most people have taken Christ out of Christmas, why not take Him out of the name?)

She jams her snoozeletters into all the cards she buys to send to friends. I just love all those cards with santas or snowmen or snow scenes on them. Ah, the true meaning of the holy day turned holiday!

She'll write something like: "George keeps busy with his job and the yard work and golf on the weekends. David is quite busy with football and friends and school. (If the woman were really honest, she would say that he was busy going to the mall, playing video games and spending his money on everything he can get his greedy little paws on!) Sherry is busy with gymnastics, piano and swimming. Joey keeps busy with his friends, soccer and baseball."

You get the busy picture.

Then with sort of a resigned sigh she'll add: "And as for me, I just try to keep everyone well-fed, happy, and on-the-go. Oh yes, Brutus our golden retriever keeps me busy, too." I wish she'd sign the letter, "Yours truly, the local busybody." Somehow it seems appropriate.

Of course, the whole point of this frenzy of activity is that while the whole family runs themselves ragged on the treadmill of busyness, they have little time for each other. Not that they really want that much time, you understand.

Better yet, they have no time to stop and think about our Adversary and His claims on their lives. And that is as it should be.

Long ago we discovered the secret that selfishness and independence are what life is all about. And if all goes well, one day we will welcome your host and his busy family into our eternal home for the terminally self-centered. Their will shall be done in hell as it was on earth. It just kind of gives you chill bumps all over, doesn't it?

By the way, many true Christian families suffer from this syndrome as much as non-Christian ones. It is the spirit of the age, my dear Spitwad, and all are vulnerable to our deception. The sweetest victory, I think, is when Christians get so busy *for* God that they become too busy for *God!*

Now closely tied in to busyness is the important idea of leading a "normal, balanced life." Of course, *we* set the agenda in the world for what a balanced life really is. This is another truth we have skillfully twisted into a half-truth.

Our Hated Creator, as you must know, designed these humans to be creative and to enjoy a wide range of healthy interests. They are encouraged by Him to develop their spirits, souls and bodies, while rejoicing in His creation. This was the terrible state of affairs we found in Eden before Our Clever Father came to the rescue.

But all the Adversary's gifts found in creation were meant to be like the spokes of a wheel, coming out from the center—a warm, joyful relationship with their heavenly Father. (I want you to know, Spitwad, that I am nearly gagging as I write this stuff!)

Alas, for your host and his family, and indeed for much of America, the hub of the wheel is gone, and so the spokes are flying everywhere in chaos and confusion. Sort of brings a lump to your throat, doesn't it?

Therefore, to your average American family, the balanced life becomes the busy life filled to the brim with nice, wholesome activities acceptable to family and friends.

Of course, just a touch of religion should be sprinkled on top for good measure, like nutmeg on top of a cup of eggnog. It adds a little flavor and makes it look nice, but don't overdo it and dump too much on or you'll ruin it.

Ah, all is well in sleepy Suburbia, is it not?

Your sleepy superior,

Slimeball

A declaration of
independence

To most worthless Spitwad,

Since you are, in kind of a weird way, a missionary to a foreign land, it is important that you stop your restless squirming for a few minutes so that you can digest some more American cultural values. I know, I know, you're anxious to get closer to your host. That time will come.

Now, if there is one foundation stone to American life that would clearly be the (pardon the expression) cornerstone of their whole existence, it would be the ideal of *freedom*.

Their national anthem says they are "the land of the free and the home of the brave." Notice when this patriotic dirge is sung at their sporting events how impatient they are for it to be finished! And how many of them actually know the words anymore? Sure there are a few diehards left who feel a sense of pride at that song, but your host is not one of them. He wouldn't know Betsy Ross from Betty Crocker!

Anyway, this American blind passion for liberty was echoed in the rallying cry of their weaning war with England: "Give me liberty or give me death!" All this freedom stuff gets pretty monotonous: Liberty Bell,

Statue of Liberty, Declaration of Independence, Independence Day, Emancipation Proclamation, etc. Even one of their states has as its motto: "Live free or die."

I have never understood this at all. Bondage is so much more fun!

Well, enough of the history lesson. I just want you to realize that most Americans have a love affair going with the concept of freedom. But as you will see, they have bought our distorted definition of freedom.

If you were to ask 100 of your host's high school buddies this question: "What is freedom?" you'd probably get 100 different answers. But in the end, most of them would say something like: "Freedom is being able to do whatever you want to do."

To your host, who sees himself as a skin-wrapped package of sex drive and salivary glands, freedom is being able to stay out as late as he wants with no curfew. I am absolutely underwhelmed!

To the invisible father of the family, freedom is playing golf without being nagged by mother to spend more time with the kids. That's really profound!

To the mother, it's having everybody out of her way for a few hours so that she can soak in her bubble bath while drinking herbal tea. Such noble patriotism!

To the modern American, freedom has simply become the selfish pursuit of personal pleasure with no one willing to say "No!" or "This is wrong!"

"Grab for all the gusto" as the old beer commercial used to say. That sums it all up pretty well.

Can you pick up the pattern? We have slyly slid the

self-centered fools away from the high concept of free-dom—away from having the ability to live and serve God without restrictions by cruel and abusive authorities. (Of course our Most Totally Worthy Master exercises his cruel and abusive control perfectly.)

Now our Adversary talks a lot about freedom in that blasted Book of His, but it all seems like a lot of mindless double-talk, if you ask me. Who would ever believe such mumbo jumbo like "the truth will set you free"?[1] Free from what? Free *for* what? I suppose He is talking about freedom from sin. But nobody *really* wants to be free from sin. It just sounds too . . . well, *dull*.

Anyway, that's the kind of stuff *He* writes about. But what gets me is that He even has the gall to turn around and expect our hosts to gladly give up the *true freedom* of "doing their own thing"! And if that weren't enough, He wants them to come to Him and do *His* thing!

"Come and be My free slave!" He says. Do you see what I mean? Who can understand such nonsense?

The craziest thing of all, Spitwad, is that those closest to the Adversary seem to enjoy it so much! In fact, His Book says of the Risen One that, "You love righteousness and hate wickedness; therefore God, your God, has set you above your companions by anointing you with the oil of joy."[2]

---

1 John 3:32 NIV
2 Psalm 45:7 NIV

Now, don't quote me on that one, Splitworm, but the mystery is that true happiness to these humans comes not from *giving in* to sin, but from *getting rid* of it! This is a secret you must guard carefully from your host's eyes. If this ever got out to all the people in the world, we would be in big trouble, because what they want more than anything else is to be happy!

Happiness coming from *holiness*? Preposterous idea! But have you ever seen the horrible (it almost seems real!) look of joy and peace and beauty on the faces of true Light-lovers? I know you have. We are indeed forever indebted to our Wonderful Master Below who has spared us from such foolishness.

But back to the subject of freedom again. We have slowly, over many years, been able to change the laws of this land. You see, in the kingdom of Light, there is no true freedom without limits. But *we* preach a different gospel—freedom with no limits!

What was once clearly wrong in America has, in many cases, become right. Or at least "a matter of opinion or preference." The bright sunlight has turned to twilight. But it has happened so slowly that only a few of the Light's watchdogs even noticed it happening.

What we eventually want to do is to make the concept of sin as old-fashioned as the eight-track tape. And then our deception will be complete. What the gullible Americans will never realize is that we will have succeeded in totally changing the meaning of the word *freedom*.

In our brave, new world the "new" freedom will simply be the *old* rebellion. When nothing is wrong anymore, then the word "sin" will simply cease to have any meaning.

Then comes the final nail in the rotting Christian coffin. If there is no sin, then there is no need for . . . you guessed it . . . a Savior! I can hardly wait!

Now, back to your host. As the lad seeks to push and squirm his way out of his childhood cocoon into adulthood, his desire for personal freedom can be a major tool for you to use.

His permissive parents basically let him do what he wants already. Without knowing it, they have painted a picture of God on the brat's mind. Bilgewater's luke-warm sermons have helped, too, of course.

"God is love" (a terrible facet of the Adversary's glory) has become "God is nice." Your host would define being nice as letting others do what they want without interfering. And so, he reasons, God must be lenient just like his parents. Your host is far from alone in coming to this conclusion, by the way. It is one of my favorite deceptions.

To attack the very character of God hits a home run almost every time. Our Shrewd Master attacked the Adversary's goodness in the Garden of Eden, making God look like a cosmic killjoy. This is a popular concept of the Adversary even today—the idea of His being a heavenly policeman. The other extreme, that God is a pampering grandfather in the sky, will work better for your host.

So, do you see how it all fits together? To the American mind, personal freedom (the pursuit of personal pleasure without restraint) becomes the new cornerstone for life. Pretty slick trick, wouldn't you agree? This kind of thinking sets your host up very nicely for his journey into "manhood." We'll deal with that delicious topic next.

But before I dismiss you, there is one more delightful detail—kind of the dessert to this whole freedom meal we've been dining on.

To preserve their so-called freedoms, Americans have created what they call "rights." *Inalienable rights* they have called them. If you remember your U.S. history lessons, the three basic rights as originally written were (and the order is very important): *life, liberty* and *the pursuit of happiness.*

That order was just another example of how the Light had infected the thinking of those revolting revolutionaries. But we have straightened it all out for them now. The inalienable rights of 20th-century America are now: *the pursuit of happiness, liberty* and *life* . . . in that order.

And so, at last, we have been able to introduce over the last few decades the very juicy idea of "a quality of life not worth living." Most people now believe this lie to be the gospel truth.

And why, dear Spitwad, would any life be deemed not worth living? Because that life somehow offends the highest goddess to be worshiped—Pursuit of Happiness.

"Death with Dignity!" "Pro Choice!" These are the rallying cries of those millions who have sacrificed at the altar of Pursuit of Happiness. Why do you think abortion clinics do such a booming business? And why do you think so many have fought so hard to stop Pro-Life protesters from hindering abortion-determined mothers from entering those clinics? Because abortion clinics are the central worship centers where the goddess *Pursuit of Happiness* is to be served!

If we have our way, many more will come crawling to us, offering their own lives or the lives of others in their extreme sickness, pain, old age or mental handicaps. In time, Dr. Kevorkian will look like Mary Poppins.

What amazes me is that the fools actually think that what awaits them on the other side of death will be pleasant. Removing the fear of death apart from the Risen One! That piece of the deception puzzle was only recently put in place. We've come a long way, baby!

Your freely superior,

Slimeball

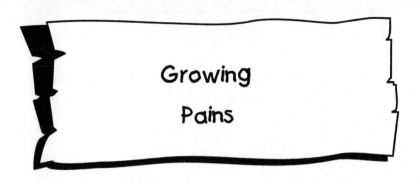

Growing
Pains

To most unworthy Spitwad,

By now you have no doubt observed that the American teenager is a most irritating and unpredictable creature. Your host's personality, for example, can be instantly changed by the appearance of a single (and nearly invisible to the naked eye) pimple on his nose. And the twerp is so vain as to think that anyone else even notices or cares! In reality, all his friends are too busy worrying about themselves to be concerned about his petty problems.

If you can believe this, Splatdrip, I have even seen the female version of the species become suddenly "ill" and miss school for several days at such an outbreak of acne. Who can ever hope to understand such behavior?

It's enough for you to realize, my dear Dimwit, that your host is obsessed with his physical body right now. Just watch him go into hysterics if he finds he's forgotten to take his comb to school! He is going through real growing pains right now. To his parents, he is a *growing pain in the neck!*

Actually, what once was just typical teen primping

has become a national pastime. Swarms of supposedly grown-up humans are grabbing for every new health and exercise fad that comes along.

The search for the fountain of youth is big business these days. And why not? If you've got nothing going for you on the inside, then you'd better make sure the outside's all pretty, right? All cleaned up and shiny and alive-looking on the outside, but dead and rotting on the inside! Just our style.

You might say that the new "seven deadly sins" of the American health, youth and beauty cult are: wrinkles, age spots, baldness, high cholesterol, high sodium, flab and sagging muscles.

Humans, of course, know nothing of true beauty, having never seen *me*.

Right now your host is far more occupied with the definition of his pectoral muscles than he is with the condition of his heart. The insecure little brat will continue to spend endless hours in the weight room. He says it is to get ready for football season (Beware, Spitwad, there is Light there!), but he's really doing it to pump up his deflated ego.

This kind of trivial pursuit is to be encouraged as much as possible. The bigger and more developed he becomes, the more easily he will be tempted to keep his eyes glued on himself in the mirror. It is only a short step from worshiping yourself to expecting others to bow down as well.

Sometime you should drop by his high school and watch the way the students relate to one another. Look carefully for the "pecking order" we have set up based on physical beauty and "coolness." How delightful it all is!

At the bottom of the ladder are the geeks who are struggling desperately to improve their social standing. That is, unless they have already given up hope of ever being "somebody."

Meanwhile, the top dogs and doggettes are nervously glancing over their shoulders, fearful that someone might come along and dethrone them. They have to work hard at maintaining their cool image. Generally these ones are so occupied with looking out for number one that they have no time to think about the *real* Number One—the One we hate. This is as it should be.

The middle class of the school just kind of carry on their humdrum lives, trying to blend in and be accepted. Theirs is an endless search for meaning and happiness in a world that yawns at anything normal.

Your host literally drools at the thought of getting to the top of the ladder. And I must give the boy some credit. He is becoming one of the most determined geeks I have ever seen.

We have done well, Spitwad, to deceive the three-dimensional creatures into living two-dimensional lives. What do I mean by that? Well, they have a physical body and a non-physical soul. And they are supposed to have a third dimension, a spirit, which is designed to contain, radiate and relate to the Light.

Most teenagers work on their physical body . . . some, and their soul . . . a little. But what about their spirit? They skip that class most of the time. How wonderful for us!

So what do they become? Instead of having depth and solidness, like three-dimensional objects, they become *flat*—like all two-dimensional objects. No depth. No purpose. Shallow. Skin deep. Dull, reflecting nothing but their own empty lives.

Your host is a classic example. He is convinced that building up his wimpy body will bring him true happiness by gaining the attention of the opposite sex and the respect of his buddies. He thinks it will make him a *man*. And in our magic kingdom, where image is everything and character means nothing, he's right. He is well on his way to becoming a manly "success." And his success will be ours as well.

You may be wondering what else your host is looking forward to as he oozes into adulthood. For one, he wants his parents to treat him like he is grown up. But not *too* grown up. He wants the freedom without the responsibility. For example, he would love to pick out what the family should have for dinner each night. But watch him throw a fit if his parents dare suggest that he help pay for the meals!

Both male and female teens have a strange love-hate relationship with their parents. It's kind of like a yo-yo—up and down, up and down. At times they want them to be close by, and at other times wish mom and dad would move to another planet!

Your host generally likes *having* his parents around, especially when he needs money or a ride somewhere.

But he doesn't like his parents *hanging* around. Do you see the difference, Spindrip? It's a matter of control. He wants them to be there only when he wants them to be there!

He wants to be able to stay out late and not come home to the parental interrogation squad. He doesn't want them prying into his private life—his phone calls, friends, mail, etc. On the other hand, he secretly wants to know that mommy and daddy care enough about him to set reasonable limits and stick to them . . . even when he screams bloody murder!

Don't try to understand all this, Spitwad. Even I am baffled at times by the teenage mind, so you shouldn't be surprised at your own confusion.

Naturally, all kinds of amusing and helpful conflicts can be exploited in your host's house. Just convince the goon that any time his parents try to talk to him about something, they are yelling at him! And any time they ask a question they are actually invading his privacy and showing they don't trust him. (Of course he never stops to consider whether he has recently given his parents any reason to trust him!) And any time his parents muster up enough courage to say no to one of his demands, they are being unfair. It's as easy as pie, Spitwad. Even you can do it.

Your host's temper tantrums and mood swings ought to drive dear ol' dad to the golf course and mother to the bubble bath even more than usual. And that's the way we want them to deal with their anger. Just so they never *really* talk.

You want to bring your host to the point where he gives up listening to his parents altogether. In time, he will be able to tune them out even when he's not wearing his headphones. A home he barely tolerates will drive him to his friends for advice. And most of his friends just happen to be our friends too. . . .

Except for that troublesome football player, Steve. He has an air about him that your host really likes. (I think it's the smell of his sweaty clothes!) He is fun-loving, but not shallow. He is confident, but not cocky. And he is respected. Unfortunately, he is also praying for your host and making it his personal project to see your host come to faith in the Light. *Steve must be stopped at all costs!*

We are working on him. He was recently voted president of the youth group at the Lighthouse. The youth pastor there is looking to him to provide a lot of leadership to that growing group. Steve tried his humble hardest to act surprised when the vote was announced, but we could tell he believed our whisper in his head: "You deserve to be elected. You are the most spiritual one here!"

We have discovered the jock's Achilles heel, the chink in his armor—spiritual pride. We will help it grow and then let it go. After all, why should we do all the work when it will gain momentum on its own.

Your smug superior,

Slimeball

Sex and the single geek

To most unworthy Spitwad,

I understand that your host has taken on a part-time job flipping burgers. His friend (who else?), Steve the Halo Head, was able to get him the job since he was so close to his sixteenth birthday. And to make matters worse, Stevie boy will be able to drive him to work since they will be working the same shift. Your host will be a captive audience—listening to the jock drone on and on about the Light, day after day. This is all your fault, Spitwad, I hope you realize that! *And* it is part of the Adversary's plot to drive us all crazy.

This job business is just another example of the restless runt's process of crawling out from under the rock of his parents' control. He is determined to get his driver's license soon, buy his own car, pay for his own insurance, and even be able to afford his own clothes!

He can't stand the thought of anyone finding out that his parents still pick out some of his clothes for him. He wants to be his own man. But in reality, he is still a slave to the approval of his buddies. Your job in this matter, Spitwad? Let him be. He's right where we want him.

Now, it's obvious from your faxes to me that you are anxious to lure your host into some of the more delicious lusts of the flesh that come with growing up—booze, drugs and sex. How long must I bear with your stupidity? Have you been hanging around Sleazedrip again? I told you he was a bad influence on you!

Haven't you figured out by now that for all your host's proud strutting around and boasting about being a "stud," he is, in many ways, still a child in a growing-up body? Deep down he's deathly afraid of becoming a man too fast. Despite all our efforts at confusing his sense of right and wrong, the Light has refused to grant us permission to completely snuff out that last faint flicker of conscience.

You jerk! Move too quickly right now and you might lose him. He could feel so overwhelmed with guilt that he might actually start listening to the jock's preaching and tumble right into the Adversary's camp! And then where would you be? You might get sent into the family gerbil or something. Hmm, what a fascinating thought. . . .

The point is, Sleazewad, that slow and steady wins the race. Let him build a nice innocent relationship with the blond floozy at church. That will keep his parents off-guard and give time for your host's hormones to erode his morals.

Don't worry about the girl. She has the moral convictions of an alley cat anyway, and she is already starting to drool over his pumped-up body. We can only hope she ignores his pumped-up ego!

Their lustful infatuation (which he thinks is true love that will last forever) will heat up fast enough without your shoving Sleazedrip's pornographic magazines and movies down his throat.

I know that all that stuff has our Master's Underworld Laboratories (UnL) seal of approval. And I know that it has helped us lure millions of men—from schoolboys to serial killers—to our Master. But your subject just might gag on it right now. In time, he will forget about spending money on clothes, believe me. Once he tastes the carnal pleasures of sin, he will gladly join the Sleazedrip Video Club.

Remember, right now he considers himself to be a good, Christian boy. His climb out of innocence and into evil must appear respectable and normal. He should see it as simply a rite of passage into manhood. Make it feel like the natural thing for two people in love.

Don't worry—that won't be as hard as it may seem now. Deep in his heart his lust is already being aroused. True, it scares him a little. But it also excites him. A few timely comments from some of the football gang in the locker room will give him the courage he needs to take the first step.

I wonder just how many teenage boys we have pushed into sex with girls by creating in them the fear that they might be gay? At least as effective as *that* motivation, is their fear of being *called* gay or fag or wuss by their peers.

Never forget, Spiderbrain, the power of a snicker or a whisper behind the back. These teens desperately want to be normal. You just make sure you're around to provide the definition of what "that" is!

I heartily encourage you to, at the right time, set the stage for the big day when the two lusters go "all the way." It can be something they look forward to for a couple of weeks. Believe me, they will think of nothing else.

Have all our favorite teenage gland-gorged, hormone-high puppets head for a weekend at the lake or something. Just so it's far enough away from the curious eyes of parents. This is the time, too, when you can introduce your host to hard booze. He's had a beer here and there but nothing like the old "demon rum." He's going to need all the help he can get to chuck the last of his inhibitions. A little boldness-in-a-bottle ought to do the trick.

But be careful. Don't let him overdo it. If he drinks too much he'll fall asleep or throw up all over everybody. That would blow the whole magical scene we are trying to create! By now he has seen so many of our movies that show sex to be the ultimate experience of life, he believes it. Your host, I don't doubt, fully expects time to move in slow motion, the atmosphere to turn kind of misty, and a saxophone to start playing in the background, when he has his first sexual experience. Like so many before him and so many after him, he has bought the whole lie—hook, line and sinker.

If you handle the situation carefully, things will run their course naturally. Their bodies will take over. I've seen it thousands and thousands of times. Oh, how delicious their sin tastes.

Encourage your host to breathe deep and long from the crystal clear air of his emerging adulthood. Let him linger long in the romantic rites that move him from boyhood to manhood. And when he looks back at his soon-to-be-buried childhood innocence, make sure a smug sneer of experience and maturity crosses his face.

And you, Spitwad, will dance with the greatest glee. For a part of your host that is precious to the Light, will have died and been swallowed up in darkness. Right in *His* face! It will be one more glorious celebration in hell!

If all works out according to plan, I might even force myself to send a flattering report to headquarters. Of course, if you blow it, I will find you. No matter where you try to hide, I *will* find you.

Your sexy superior,

Slimeball

Leaven's street-cleaning business

To most unworthy Spitwad,

I have been poking around a bit to find out what Leaven is up to in our jurisdiction. It's been too ghastly quiet, and that makes me nervous. So here's the latest scoop.

I trust you have been following the progress of the late-breaking story of the kidnapping of teenage prostitutes in the city? This has been going on for quite a while, you know.

Kids run away from home and foolishly run right into the arms of an abusive city. They come to us so innocent and fragile. It only takes a few weeks in our school of hard knocks—the streets—before they find themselves tough and hard. At least on the outside. That's how they survive and keep the city from chewing them up and spitting them out.

Desperate for money and love they sell their bodies to the first bidder. And they sell their souls to the streets . . . and to us.

Anyway, the girls and boys on the street have been scared silly for months, but no one was talking. That is, until recently. A squealer has gone to the cops pleading for protection. He spilled the whole story

58

as well as he could from the evidence he's pieced together.

He told them that occasionally, either a plain, gray four-door or dark blue mid-size sedan pulls up and a street-walker climbs in and is never seen or heard from again.

Luckily, the license plate numbers he wrote down and gave to the cops will prove to be a dead end. Leaven is too smart for that. Besides, how long are the cops going to bother looking for a few missing runaways? Not long. Leaven will see to that.

So, unfortunately, our friends will simply have to lay low and find another source of bodies for their midnight parties in the woods. And they will. Eclipse, I hear, is never satisfied. Leaven will oblige him. They always do. They have no choice.

Your superior snoop,

Slimeball

Go jump
in a lake!

To most unworthy Spitwad,

I f I didn't have the hard, cold evidence right here in front of me—the latest report of your tiresome bungling—I would not believe it possible! One of *my* demons managed to turn the perfect setup into a total disaster. Oh, your claims of being ignorant and innocent are quite well written. And, in part, I do believe them. For you are without a doubt the most *ignorant* being ever created!

"How could I know," you plead, "that the weekend of the trip to the lake would also be the weekend of my host's grandmother's birthday party?" How could you know? How could you not know! *It is your business to know, you idiot!*

Did it not occur to you that things like restaurant reservations, invitations, buying gifts, etc. meant that some special event was coming up? And did it never occur to you to check the date of that special event, you infernal fool?

Do you realize that you and I came within a spider's thread of being turned over to the torturers? As it is, I have been assigned the task of cleaning all the latrines in hell for a week. And guess who's going to do the work for me? You guessed it, toiletbreath! And guess whose toothbrush we're going to use? Right again! But then, I would have to stay with you to make sure you didn't accidentally (out of ignorance and innocence, of course!) melt the stupid polar ice cap!

And so the weary drama of your misdeeds continues. Despite your host's frantic pleadings to escape with his lusty friends to the lake, his parents would not hear of it. What a time for Mr. and Mrs. Permissive to lay down the law!

Why were they so dead set against your host missing the party? *Why*, you ask? Are you so completely dense as to forget that this grandmother is still praying? In fact, it's getting worse. She seems to do little else. Oh, what have I ever done to deserve this kind of irritation?

It was a well-deserved torture for you, though, to have to endure that old woman's 30-minute testimony of her life with the Light. I just couldn't believe that the rest of her family let her get away with doing that. The cowards! There they sat like obedient little schoolchildren listening to her rattle off verses from that hated Book. It was like spiritual artillery fire booming against the walls of our strongholds!

That would have been bad enough, but then *He* showed up. That Unwelcome Intruder took the opportunity to pour out such power, love, and joy upon her voice and face that even at this distance I had to cover my ears and eyes!

If not for your host's father wheeling in the cake at

just the right moment, the whole room full of them might have been converted. As it was, 75 burning candles on the cake provided the needed distraction to break the mood.

But, of course, the old woman had to sneak in one final comment: "Unlike these small flames, which so easily are blown out, the fire of God's love and power in my heart can never be snuffed out. In fact, it only burns brighter and stronger as I see Him drawing near." How sickening!

By the way, your miserable screams of pain and terror were most unprofessional and unbecoming to an apprentice of mine. You gave far too much opportunity for those goody-two-shoes angels to rejoice.

You are now the laughingstock of the entire spiritual world. I hope you are quite proud of yourself. Don't you see how bad this makes *me* look?

And, to top it all off, your host was impressed by the whole scene. Don't be a fool, Spitwad! What sounds like syrupy slop to us is just the sort of thing these sentimental humans remember. The following morning, Sunday, as Bilgewater was blurting out his usual bloated blasts of hot air, the brat was in deep thought. He was probably comparing the power of his grandmother's preaching to that pompous puffball in the pulpit. Disturbing questions formed in his mind. Believe me, anytime your host thinks deeply about *anything,* you can be sure that the Light is lurking somewhere nearby.

Without the distracting presence of the blond bombshell, he actually came very close to praying! Beware Spitball!

By the way, in case you haven't heard, the girl ditched your host since he couldn't go to the lake, and she hooked up with a senior football player on steroids. Bigger body, smaller brain—sounds like her type.

This plague of prayer must be stopped immediately! A terrible shiver rattled all through hell Saturday night as a frightening roar of triumph and joy exploded from heaven. And it was your fault!

As a result of granny's sermon, your host's little brother was lost. That's right, Spitdrip, Spatwart, or whatever your name is. He's lost to the Light forever!

Our Adversary is surrounding your host with Light-lovers. Granny, that jock, Steve, and now there's even one in *your* house. We must retaliate swiftly and furiously. Do you understand? No, I don't mean the new little traitor. We have other agents far more efficient than you who will deal with that piece of fungus.

Besides, with your track record, you'd probably turn him into the next apostle Paul in three months! Your host's brother happens to be heavily guarded by the Light right now, anyway.

No, my fortunate apprentice, something else has

happened that concerns you and your host. Something even more tasty than the sin of sex. It happened at the lake—with a little help from our friends. This is what really saved you from Penguinland, something more in your realm of experience.

Due to the great brilliance of MindInvader (one of *my* former trainees who actually listened to me!), things are looking better for us. MindInvader, you might like to know, has connections to Eclipse. Or so rumor has it.

Here's what happened. Some of our dear, dear friends who have come through our door and thrown away the key joined the orgy at the lake. One of them just happens to be the teenage son of a rather important government official who just happens to have a keen interest in teenage runaways. Get the picture?

Anyway, at the lake they told some rather juicy stories of their experiences with us. Of course, these prophets of ours are convinced that we are not demons. They think we are the disincarnate spirit guides of wise gurus. We have totally deceived them into thinking that they are merely discovering the hidden powers of their own minds. In reality, they are out of their minds, and *we are in!*

The whole teenage brood is quite curious about it all, and you *will* make sure that the little mouse, AKA your host, joins in and enters the playground of the cat. But this kitty is actually a roaming lion looking for teenage geeks to devour! He is smacking his lips even now.

After all, this *is* supposed to be your area of training.

I demand great reports of your progress. You won't disappoint me again now, will you?

We must teach the Adversary a painful lesson here. He must know that every move He makes will be matched by us with an even more vicious counterattack.

But, oh, beware Spitwad. Not all is well in snoring Suburbia tonight. For Light-lover Steve and that old woman still pray. And now they are not alone.

Your furious and curious superior,

Slimeball

Sweet revenge

To most unworthy Spitwad,

I understand that the mood around your house has been wonderfully dark and depressed lately. The poor lad continues to mope around with a black cloud of "woe is me" hanging over his head. He doesn't even notice that no one comes to his pity party anymore. How sad.

The sulking child is so intimidated by his ex-girlfriend and her steroid-stud boyfriend that he can't bring himself to tell her how much he is hurting. But, oh, Spitwad, this is some of the most delicious gourmet dining for you! Make sure you savor all the delicious flavors of his bitterness, as the poison silently and steadily spreads throughout his soul.

How many times is it now, I wonder, that he has pushed the play and rewind buttons on his mental VCR? Over and over again he relives that scene when she tossed her head and announced she was going to the lake without him. Each time he plays that videotape, his anger grows stronger and more sour.

Though it would have been nice if your host had been allowed to go to the lake, much good has come from this turn of events already. I will treasure forever that precious look of rejection on your poor puppy's face when the blond flirt turned and marched away from him. You could see his whole self-esteem shatter into a million pieces and come crashing to the ground.

I hear he has quit his job, thus effectively isolating him from that irritating friend of his, Steve. And he's even stopped lifting weights, since steroid boy practically lives in the weight room.

By now, plenty of suns have gone down on his anger. You were anxious to get closer to your host, weren't you? Well, here's your chance.

I heartily encourage you to keep a steady stream of fresh venomous thoughts flowing into his mind. Have you tried this one: "I hope she gets some kind of disease from the jerk! On second thought, she'll probably give it to *him*!" Or "After all I did for her (which actually means, 'After all the money I spent on her') and all the good times we had, I can't believe she used me like that. She's not going to get away with it, that's all I can say!"

Make sure, Splatworm, that *is* all he can say. We want his bitterness to fully ripen and consume him. His friends, of course, will all be on his side. They will help your poison continue to course through his veins.

It is time now, Spitwad, for you to snap him out of his depression. He spends all his free time alone, and that has served its purpose. Now he is ready for the next step. He has gotten mad; now he needs to get even.

He will recover very quickly from his depression once revenge becomes his new reason for living. He will need your help, however, in coming up with a plan of action. Needless to say (but then, with you there is *nothing* that is "needless to say"), he must have no idea that you exist or that you are suggesting ideas to him. He must be convinced that *your* ideas are actually *his* ideas.

When you whisper your sweet nothings into his mind, say it like this: "Hmm, let's see. Oh, I've got a great idea! Yeah, I know what I'll do." The fool will be so proud of himself that he'll never stop to really wonder where that brilliant idea actually came from!

Once again, at least for now, you will be most effective if you remain totally hidden. Be patient; that will change. Believe me, the time is coming when you will be able to dance in the light.

It would be valuable, I think, for me to spend a little time reminding you of the power of three of our friends: *misunderstanding, hurt feelings* and *unforgiveness.*

The Light deals with the cowardly way of *apology, mercy* and *forgiveness.* Anyone can forgive someone else. That is the tasteless diet of weaklings. It takes a person with strength and courage to nurse a grudge and not give it up, if you ask me!

Humans are constantly misunderstanding each other. It is, of course, because they don't care enough about one another to really listen. They're too proud. They quickly decide that they fully understand what the other person really means, really feels, or really needs. Nine times out of ten, however, they are dead wrong.

Take, for example, your host's parents. The play develops like this:

Act One

Misunderstanding. Mother has had a horrid day with the three brats. Two of them, as usual, needed rides to their endless activities while the third was whining about a stomachache. The poor sick creature was then unable to make it to the toilet in time and so launched a very gross glob onto the new carpet. It created a most interesting (and smelly!) stain.

To add insult to illness, report cards just came out and it's "read 'em and weep" time.

The stage is set. Enter the man of the house. He has been trying hard all day to make people like his ideas in a high-pressure board-room meeting. It was not a pleasant scene. He is exhausted and frustrated and has high hopes that he will find Cleopatra herself waiting for him with open arms, lips, and a romantic dinner. After all, it *is* Friday night. But instead he finds the Wicked Witch of the West down on her knees angrily scrubbing the carpet.

Romeo turns quickly into Attila the Hun as he demands, "What have you been doing all day? The house is a mess, the kid is moaning, the new carpet is ruined and there's no dinner on the table!"

Need I say more? The lightning bolts from Cleo's eyes tell the story.

Act Two

Hurt feelings. Romeo, his sexy mood destroyed, storms out the door saying in his usual sensitive, kind way, "I'm going down to the bar and have a few drinks with the guys! At least *they* understand what hard work is all about!"

I couldn't have said it better myself.

Her lightning bolts quickly fizzle out into a heavy downpour, leaving puddles of tears all over the carpet.

(Such a wonderful mess! I'm talking about their marriage, Spitwad, not the rug.

Now it's important at this critical point that you move in fast. Remind them of how hurt they feel and that all of it is the other person's fault. By inflating their egos like this, you can guard against the Light. He will try to stir up feelings of sorrow or . . . Satan forbid . . . repentance. If you play your cards right, the drama will continue on.)

Act Three

Unforgiveness. The hubby, of course, was in the wrong. This time anyway. But don't let it dawn on him that maybe he spoke just a little too quickly when he barged into the house, demanding that his needs be met.

His drinking buddies will help bolster his pride by reminding him, "Yeah, women. All they do all day is watch soaps, eat chocolates, and get fat." And, "Dames. You can't live with 'em and you can't live without 'em. But I'm trying." That line will no doubt be followed by a lot of burping, laughing, and slapping each other on the back.

(Most of those boozing bozos have spent more time at the bar and in divorce court than in school. So you can imagine the quality of marriage advice he'll pick up there!)

Meanwhile, back at the ranch, mother dear has gathered herself bravely together and has begun to prepare dinner (at least for the children, she sniffs). She is already a master of the cold shoulder/silent treatment. He hates that and she knows it. She already has the chilly reception rehearsed in her mind for when the drunken bum finally staggers in.

If he doesn't come crawling back to her, full of apologies, she will turn the thermostat down to a deep chill for as long as necessary. The children side with her; they always do. Eventually he will break; he always does.

And so, my slimy slave, your host has learned how to take sweet revenge from his parents. Of course, he has already been involved in one form of vengeance—the mental kind.

Misunderstanding the fickle flirt and being convinced he was the only one for her, his fragile feelings were deeply wounded when she ditched him. Unforgiveness quickly followed as he angrily and jealously beat her and whipped her over and over again on the movie screen of his mind.

Now *we* know that the thing that *really* eats him alive is that she deprived him of the one thing that he feels would make him a real man—in his eyes and in the eyes of his friends. Sex. Lust that is aroused and then cheated out of its prize is like the fading mirage of an oasis in the desert to a man dying of thirst. It drives him mad.

First, of course, your host will parade around school with his head held high, proudly declaring that he is now over her. Everyone will think him strong and tough for having endured what he did. They will gladly listen again as he tells of his suffering and pain. But, he will assure them, it is all ancient history now.

You will help train him in the fine art of false-hood—to be able to look someone straight in the eye and tell him a bald-faced lie without flinching takes time and practice. He must learn that lying to get what he wants is necessary to make it to the top. Show him that honesty is *not* the best policy . . . point to any politician!

Of course, we know that he is nowhere near over her. But we won't tell now, will we?

The normal way of revenge in a case like this, would be to launch a direct verbal attack on the blond's reputation. That's a dead end in this case. She has no reputation worth attacking. There must be another way . . . and there is.

The girl's mother refuses to believe that her daughter is anything but an innocent church girl. Mother Ostrich has buried her head in the sand for years over a number of things, Spitwad. But to our advantage, she somehow has come to love and trust your host.

One day you should have him casually drop by to see her (at a time when he knows the girl will be out), just to say hi. She will be delighted, for she is a lonely woman. During the course of his visit, he should tell her that he feels it is his duty to warn her about her daughter's *new friend*. He must come across as very sincere and noble at this point. She will not suspect him at all.

Your host should ask the mother to keep his visit a secret and not tell her daughter. He should say that he feels this act of "kindness" would somehow be spoiled if she knew. As he leaves, let him remind her that he simply felt it was the "loving thing to do"—to do all he could to save "Sweet Polly" from the clutches of such a fiend.

Mother dear will be horrified at the news, but deeply grateful to your host for opening her eyes. And so she will swallow the whole pile of manure, and state that she will forbid the girl from seeing steroid-man again. Have your host say, with a serious nod of his head, that that would probably be best for everyone.

And then he will literally explode with hateful glee once he leaves her house and walks down the block.

You see, Spitwad, if the girl has one bad quality (which in this case is to our advantage), she has such pity for her mother that she has vowed never to do anything to hurt her.

That's why she has kept her current relationship a secret. And that is why she will obey her mom! The vengeful one knew that all along. He is learning well, using everything to his advantage. Such a good Christian boy.

Do you see how simple it all is? We have split up the best of friends, divided families, and even sliced in half some of the Adversary's most dangerous churches this way.

Remember the recipe: Mix equal parts *misunderstanding* and *hurt feelings*. Fold in several cups of pride and whip rapidly to prevent settling and guilt feelings. Bake in the oven of *unforgiveness* until hard and crusty. Its taste will be quite bitter if done properly. Frost generously with heaping spoonfuls of jealousy and revenge.

So there you have it. You see, my dull Spitwad, you *can* have your cake and eat it, too. Just make sure no one along the way decides to eat humble pie instead. That stuff leaves a sickly sweet taste in the mouth, and always causes our cakes to fall before they're done. Good eating!

Your drooling superior,

Slimeball

Being bored
to death

I was pleased, though not at all surprised, to hear that my plan for your host's much-deserved revenge was warmly received by him. He must have performed quite well, because the yellow-haired floozy's mother thanked him over and over for his unselfish act of mercy.

The furious shrieks of the fickle little flirt could be heard all the way down here when mommy dearest slammed the door on steroid-boy. I wonder what really angered the girl more—not being able to have his body or not having the social status that being seen with him brought her?

Her sobbing cries of "Why? Why? Why?" almost bullied Mrs. Ostrich into ratting on your rat. That would not have been so bad, now that I think about it.

But her mother was resourceful enough to pull out her report card, shove it in her face, and announce to her that *that* was why she was being grounded. How could the girl argue? Her report card looked like a Sesame Street lesson on the letters D and F!

Your host's glad triumph, however, has already worn off. Revenge, if you haven't noticed, is simply another one of our Master's appealing but disappointingly empty meals. It's kind of like Chinese food. It smells great while you're waiting for it, and tastes great while you're eating it, but in a little while you're hungry again.

Your spoiled brat is already feeling bored. And that is to be expected. Since his most recent days have been spent worshiping his female fantasy, he's not quite sure what to do with himself.

Being of limited intelligence, as you are, Spitwad, you may find it hard to believe that your host could possibly be bored. After all, he attends school, works (I heard that Steve, the jock, lured him back into that job), and works out over at the dweeb Steve's house. And whatever free time your boy scrapes together is spent involved in some other unfulfilling pursuit.

You must try hard to understand something, my slow-to-learn apprentice. With humans, the fact that they are busy does not mean they aren't bored.

There is, to be sure, the type of boredom that comes from having nothing to do and no one to do it with. Our close friends in prison solitary confinement and many of our victims in nursing homes and hospitals live this way. They exist in the empty, aching, colorless world of loneliness. Hopeless boredom of this sort is often our method of reward for a lifetime of hard work.

There is another type of boredom, too. It is the agonizing repetition of labor in some factories and work camps. This boredom comes from feeling under-challenged, trapped, and hopeless. A milder version of this can be seen if you visit a hot, stuffy, classroom right after lunch on a sunny, spring day. The teacher keeps droning on and on, totally unaware of the tortured yawns and longing looks out the window from his captive students.

By the way, have you ever had the bad luck to hear Bloatwart boast about how he introduced the saying, "God helps those who help themselves" to America? Better than a sleeping pill any day!

Anyway, your host's problem with boredom is none of the above. You see, up until his "great divorce" with the "Run Around Sue," he was excited about what he called "life." Why? Because every one of his five senses and nearly all of his hormones were in overdrive. His nerves were literally tingling with the pleasure and excitement of it all—kind of like riding a motorcycle out in the warm sunshine of the open highway for the first time.

But now, the poor little child finds himself peddling his tricycle in the back yard again. All the excitement and fun are gone because his girl is gone and life is *bor*-ing!

To the American teen who is raised on a steady diet of action, excitement, and entertainment, life in the slow lane brings some pretty intense boredom. Oh, the world can be so unfair! Boo hoo, sniff, sniff . . .

Well, Spitwad, of what use is all of this to us? First, you must convince your host that his boredom is always someone else's fault, never his own. Encourage him to let out his frustration and restlessness with statements like, "This school stinks" or "That teacher is so dull" or "Math really bores me." Let it never dawn on him that the real problem might be that *he* is boring!

In this case, my simple Spitwad, boredom is our friend. Since more excitement is what he is after, give it to him. It will be easy to lure him into more and more, and deeper and deeper, traps of the flesh and the world . . . always searching for the perfect high, the greatest ecstasy.

Experiences, thrills and excitement can easily become like an addictive drug. But today's rush quickly grows old and cold and becomes tomorrow's boredom. He will then be fair game for the next temptation and the next and the next. If all goes according to plan, we can keep the fool stumbling around, groping for the final, true satisfaction that strangely eludes him, for years.

You see, there is something much deeper and more central going on here. Your host and his bored buddies are missing the light of life. They were "bred" to graze in the green pastures of the Adversary, seeking their ultimate joy in knowing *Him* and doing what pleases *Him*. But we've got them now, trapped in *our* empty stables, chewing the tasteless straw we provide, and doing what pleases *us*.

They have a vague sense that there's something more to life, but since all they see are other bored animals doing the same thing, they don't really look around very hard. Drinking, partying, doing drugs, sleeping around, etc. keep their brains numb enough, their eyes cloudy enough, and their hearts hard enough to keep them from finding the way out. We've got them where we want them!

They're too busy convincing themselves and each other that they're having fun. It never dawns on them to question what awaits them. We have done a masterful job! Day by day the human cattle shuffle nearer and nearer to the slaughterhouse.

But beware, Spitwad! Boredom can also become our enemy. It can turn on us and become a window through which the soul can see its own emptiness. Sometimes people who have spent many years with us suddenly wake up, blow away the cobwebs, open up the curtains, and wonder why they never went outside into the sunshine before.

This is one of the most frustrating tactics of the Light. I hate it when he turns our weapons against us!

That football hero, Steve, is not helping matters any. He has this terrible character quality—he seems to sincerely love your host. Every time he picks your host up for work after one of his drunken binges, he just smiles at him and treats him with nauseating respect. The jock-jerk acts as if the piece of trash were somehow a *valuable* person! Time after time your host cringes as he climbs into the car, expecting to be verbally ripped to shreds by Little Boy Christian. But it never happens. This is deeply disturbing and totally unacceptable. I'm afraid we are up against *grace*, my dear Spitwad, and the Light is starting to shine powerfully on your host.

So, before your human specimen has time to discover that there is something or Someone missing from his life, let's offer him a *real* experience. That's what he wants anyway—something that will tingle his senses, amaze his mind, and explode his emotions. Something mysterious, eerie, and powerful. Something that only the "chosen ones" can have.

Are you getting the message, Splitwit? It's time to introduce your mouse to the playground of the cat.

Your sinister superior,

Slimeball

Fun and games in the New Age

To most unworthy Spitwad,

I suppose I have to bring you up to speed on our latest-and-greatest New Age innovations. I sure wish your tiny brain could keep up with the times! Anyway, the doors into our lair are numerous, as you know, and these Americans practically trample each other in order to rush through them. They pride themselves on not being gullible or easily faked out, but we do it to them all the time!

Just look at the hundreds and thousands of dollars they fork over to hear words from "the other side." It is all such fun—change the name and fool the public! "Medium" was so old-fashioned and a little scary-sounding, so we changed the name to "channeler"—and now they suddenly are the rage! Nobody wants to be possessed by a demon, so now we call ourselves spirit guides, and everybody wants us!

Personally, I don't care what they call us, just so they put out the welcome mat! And they have!

The humans are even convinced that they can tap into some mysterious cosmic energy by hanging a crystal around their necks! It's a rather convenient collar (or should I say noose) for our pets, wouldn't you say?

Horoscopes, Ouija boards and Tarot cards have successfully ensnared the human insects in our web for years. And we have many other fortune-telling aids in our catalog as well.

For the youthful audience, we have our full assortment of fantasy role-playing games. Whether they're played on a computer, a TV set or a board doesn't matter. We introduce them to the wonderful world of spells, potions, powers, gods, demigods, incantations, secret writings, rape, murder, theft and violence.

My ears love to hear the proud protests of those who play these games: "Aw, it's just a harmless game!" The fact of the matter is that, for many, the games become the most exciting part of their lives. Their real lives are so dull that they find increasing pleasure and excitement by retreating into our fantasy world where they feel important. That factor alone is enough to put the games on our bestseller list.

But there is more. The young innocents fail to understand that the games are ours—and that we're drawing them away from the Holy One. What an accomplishment! Even the Christian kids justify themselves! We help, of course, by reminding them that "it's all in fun" (*our* kind of fun, that is!).

The young Light-lovers never cease to amaze me. One minute they're watching a cheap Christian TV program and the next minute they're chopping off someone's head in a video game! And then they scratch their heads and wonder why their relationships with God are so dull and boring.

Thankfully, there are precious few who figure out that our games are really a door into the occult. By then, many find that that's what they wanted all along. Then they're ready for the real thing. And we gladly give it to them!

Once again, Spitwad, be careful and don't move too fast. You don't want to frighten your host away. Just a gentle nudge down the slippery slope of the occult is all he needs. Don't push him too hard. Let him read some of our more scientific-looking magazine stories about visualization and guide imagery. Let him chew on some of the more Christian-sounding "wisdom" from our spirit guides.

I suggest you gradually introduce him to the idea of having his own personal spirit guide. After all, this is a difficult and confusing time for him. What better way to make it through than to tap into the wisdom of the ages?

Make sure one of our human preachers introduces himself warmly to him. Have him share a "testimony" of some practical, down-to-earth insights that his guide has given him. (And oh how short a journey it is, Spitwad, from being a *guide* to becoming a *god*!)

Halloween will soon be upon us. (By the way, have you finished your shopping yet, Spendthrift? As usual, last year you waited until the last minute and then spent all your money on stupid gifts for yourself. How rude! Wait till you see what I got for *myself* this year. You will be green with envy!)

Take advantage of the holiday season. Certainly

you should be able to arrange an innocent little party for your hosts and friends¿ Make sure the mood is right—spooky and fun, but not overtly evil. You know what I mean. Then perhaps you could arrange for some of our teenage New Age "evangelists" to show up around 11:30 P.M.

They could maybe give a little "sermon" and then have our type of altar call. And when your host opens his heart to us, you will be right there to accept his invitation. Then the two of you could spend as much time together as you like. *Spitwad the spirit guide.* Oh well, I suppose it will have to do.

Trick or treat!

Your superiorly supernatural,

Slimeball

The holiday spirit

To most worthless Spitwad,

Ah, Spitwad, this is my favorite time of the year. The days are getting shorter, the nights longer. The warmth of summer is long gone and the chill winds of fall are blowing. The trees are losing their leaves and soon the entire landscape will be bleak, brown and desolate. Such beauty!

Yes, the Halloween season is upon us. Don't you just love all the beautiful decorations—black cats, spiders, bats, witches, ghosts, goblins, and pumpkins with scary faces? I can barely contain myself when all the little humans dress up like vampires, aliens and other hideous monsters. Some of those masks even startle me a bit.

Watching the greedy little candy grabbers go door to door, hoping to find a real spooky house (with good candy of course) brings a lump to my throat. A fascination with fear, an interest in the supernatural and curiosity about the dark side of life really plays into our hands, doesn't it? After all, evil is "in" these days, isn't it?

Halloween, our highest holy day, is prime time for

all kinds of fun and games for Leaven as well. I understand they have agents lurking around haunted houses and amusement park "fright nights" in order to recruit children and teenagers. After all, this is the perfect time of year and the perfect time to introduce curious and naive ones to the mysteries of darkness.

You see, Sputterwaff, we really don't care what motivations the human pests have for dabbling in the dark side.

Some of them even think it's all a game. And we'll gladly play along. Some are just a little bit curious. We'll let them sniff a whiff of the supernatural—just enough to start them drooling. Some know what we offer and they're hungry. We'll quickly draw them into the fold.

Whether they merely crack the door to our domain of darkness a wee bit or throw it wide open, we are well-pleased. Either way, they have chosen to take a walk on the wild side—our side.

Remember our favorite stay-with-us line? "Once you've tasted the forbidden fruit, you can never go back again." Of course, that's not really true—but they don't know that. You and I both know the horrible truth: that while any human still has life and breath there is always the chance for that hated repentance. But will we let on?

You may be wondering, on this most glorious Halloween, how our human agents get their pointy little claws into the young and tender ones? One tried and true method is drugs. Now, your host, at this point in his pagan pilgrimage, is far too straight-laced to swallow this pill. But many adolescents—in the right place with the proper dose of peer pressure—will try anything once. Get one of the teen punks high and watch their thirst for higher and mightier thrills and chills kick into overdrive! And who is more "high and mighty" than us?

How else will the Leaven-agents try to attract new converts? Well, even you, Spitwad, should be able to figure this one out. Many teenagers today are marvelously aching and empty on the inside. They long for a sense of belonging—having been physically, mentally and emotionally used, misused and abused at home. They are like sitting ducks for us. How? One way is gangs. Gangs provide a home and family to the poor wayward waifs. A sense of identity. A place of power. A place where we have great influence.

Although some gangs are training grounds for future Leavenites, many are not. But do we care? If a kid learns that "laws are meant to be broken," "a gun in your hand means power," "those outside 'the family' are enemies" and "money buys happiness," we have accomplished our purpose.

So, I say, let the bad times

roll! May chaos, havoc, deception, fear, violence, horror, hatred and death rule! This is our night, so let us revel in it! Ah, how delightful to feel that holiday spirit once again.

And tonight, Spitwad, is also the night that your host goes to that innocent little Halloween party. This is your big chance! I know you're excited but try not to slobber too much on your Bugs Bunny costume. I look forward to hearing about your inside job.

Jack O'Slimeball

To most worthless Spitwad,

Speaking of children, you should know about another development in your town. And since you only read the comics in the daily newspaper, chances are you are clueless about the latest news.

An abortion clinic has just opened up in the community. Recent laws passed against protesters have encouraged the market a bit, after all those ugly incidents in recent years. I really can't imagine why there was all the fuss anyway. You would think we were running some sort of death camp or something!

This clinic, like all abortion clinics, is being supervised by a strong man, a "high official" in our army, a ruler on the level with Eclipse. Who is he, Spitslurp? His code name is Molech. He's been around for a good while, but now he has decided to join forces with Eclipse.

Eclipse loves money and needs money for his purposes. Molech loves children and needs children for his purposes. A marriage made in hell. How lovely.

Your host, being in his prime lustbucket years, could one day provide some business for the local abortion clinic. The school-fools have opened up a new "health clinic" in his high school and he has already grabbed a fistful of condoms—just in case. I know that you are shocked and deeply disappointed, Spitwad, to find out they're not balloons! If it weren't for your utter stupidity, you might actually be amusing.

Anyway, this is where "the rubber meets the road." If we play our cards right and the right girl comes along, who knows? Think of all the pregnant possibilities! Even you should be able to get your host to buy the "safe sex" lie. That will encourage him to go for it. Then, in the heat of passion, he will easily become careless with his "protection." You might say the lust-fool will become con*dumb*.

By the way, isn't it amazing what we have done with words? The Supreme Serpent himself claims responsibility for coining the term *pro-choice*. And I don't doubt it. It sounds so . . . so . . . American. So open and tolerant. And so deceptive. Plenty of choice for the woman; no choice for the baby!

The same thing goes for the term *right to privacy*. Molech says he came up with that one. And the beautiful side of this evil is that people will fiercely debate and defend this so-called "right." Why? Because it lies at the very heart of what it means to be in control of one's own life. They lie at the very heart of what it means to be a sinner.

"Take your laws off my body!" "Don't bring your morality into my bedroom!" "I'll never go back!"—these and other slogans the pro-abortion people shout are pure and simple rebellion against the Light. They cling desperately to what they think the Constitution says, and completely ignore the Adversary's Book! *That's the way, uh huh, uh huh, we like it!*

And that's why we demons always have been and always will be 100% pro-choice! We know, of course, that pro-choice means *pro-abortion.* The false promise of relief and freedom to the mother becomes a sentence of death for the child. And that's why Molech took on this job back in the 60's. He's always had a special place in his heart for children.

Already the abortion clinic in your town is doing a booming business. Your host passes by it every day on his way home from school. He cranes his neck to see if he can recognize any of the poor, frightened females who slink in and out of there each day. Meanwhile, inside the doctors and nurses keep on raking in the bucks even as they rake out the babies. Hmm, doesn't it say something in the Adversary's book about the love of money being the root of all sorts of evil? Quite so. That's one truth even I can accept—and use to our advantage!

The supreme irony of all this abortion clinic hubbub is that the law punishes someone convicted of murdering a doctor who performs abortions; but those who murder unborn children through abortion are protected by law!

I don't even think our All-Cunning master below could have anticipated how deep into the darkness America would sink. Just thinking about it all makes me drunk with delight.

And, unless one of those stinking, ghastly revivals takes place, we ain't seen nothin' yet, baby!

Your clinically superior,

Slimeball

The greatest disaster since the Titanic

To most unbelievably inept Spitwad,

Bunglers! Brainless, moldy-minded morons! Witless, senseless imbeciles! Why don't MindDistracter and his stumbling, bumbling brood just step right up to the Adversary Himself and ask what would best serve His cause? That couldn't possibly be any worse than what they have already accomplished! Better yet—maybe the whole slimy brood of them should join HeartFreezer. They deserve each other.

When I received the complete report, Spitwad, I fully expected that you would be the one to blame as usual. Officially, you have been cleared. But *I* wonder. . . . It never ceases to amaze me how you always seem to be nearby when disaster strikes. I'm actually beginning to believe our deceptions about superstitions and jinxes and bad luck—*because of you*.

The Halloween party was going just as planned. It couldn't have been more ideal. Interest in our little magical, mystery tour was running high—MindInvader and his teenage prophets were spinning their web to perfection. Your host was fascinated by all the power and knowledge available to him.

So, they were just about to join hands and begin the seance when the cursed phone rang! Didn't I warn you about that? Didn't you have someone take it off the hook? I'm sure I told you to do that. That was an oversight that will be thoroughly investigated. Make no mistake about that!

"It's for you," the girl whispered to your host. Didn't you suspect that something was up? Of course you didn't, you dingbat!

You could have planted the thought in your host's mind to get the girl to lie and tell the caller he wasn't there. Or you could have interfered with the phone lines. Anything! But no, you were as curious as the rest of them, and so you sat there like a perfect ninny and listened in!

If only I hadn't been called away to disrupt an annoying gathering of young Light-lovers over at that meddler Steve's house. I would have instantly taken charge of your situation and saved the day.

But something had to be done about that gathering. They called it a hallelujah party; I called it one major headache. Of all the nerve—they scheduled an evening of worship and prayer on our sacred night of Halloween! It was simply too much to endure. Somebody had to move in to stop the prayer. Naturally, I was the one called in to help.

Ah, but now I can see the Light's strategy clearly. It was all a huge set-up job. Crude, but effective. It's a good thing our EverAlert Master sensed the trap and issued the alarm to all demons before all heaven broke loose on us.

But that awful hallelujah party. And that terrible, terrible singing and praying! Our minds were staggering from it all. The warning from below didn't reach MindDistracter in time.

Someone will pay for that slip up.

An official protest to the Adversary's secretary has already been made. But it won't do any good. It never does. I can almost see the smug smile of satisfaction on *His* face. It's bad enough that He wrecks our plans, but on Halloween? Is nothing sacred anymore?

And so MindDistracter was cut off from all help, and he was too drunk on his own self-importance and too blinded by his own anger to even notice that he was walking into a trap.

He was at the old, praying woman's house doing everything his muddled brain could think of to stop her. But she just kept on and on, singing and praying for your host and for all the brats that came to her door. "God bless you," she had to say as she gave them each candy and a gospel tract.

Then when the confusion in our ranks was at its peak, the Adversary's trap was sprung. The Light's angelic goons left granny's side for just the briefest moment—and MindDistracter's chief idiot, Life-Crusher, out of pure reflex, saw his opening and struck.

"We had waited 62 years for a chance like that," was his whining excuse. He acted on impulse, not on reason. Tsk tsk. He will have an eternity in flames to rethink that move.

It was 11:45 P.M. The praying woman slumped to

the ground having suffered massive cardiac arrest. But she remained conscious long enough (no doubt a result of the Adversary's hand) to place a phone call to your host's house. Then came the ambulance, the hospital emergency room and ICU.

The mood and the moment at the Halloween party were shattered by that phone call. "It's my mom. I've gotta go. She says my grandma has had a really bad heart attack and an ambulance is coming to take her to the hospital. Sorry."

And then your host threw the phone down and was out the door, running home. Did you happen to go with him, Spitwad, or did you decide to stay and enjoy the party some more, you idiot!

The whole thing was a clever plot designed to rescue your host's miserable soul from our clutches. Can't you see? It was the bold move of the Adversary that I warned you about.

It's beyond me, though, why the Heavenly Meddler even bothers with him. That piece of teenage trash cares nothing for Him. It's simply an absurd waste of energy on the Light's part. And I've seen Him do it over and over again.

It seems like such a crazy idea that I can scarcely imagine it. And yet the Adversary is famous for His twisted logic. Spitwad, it seems He felt it was a good bargain to sacrifice the praying woman in order to save hormone head.

Our Worthy Master rightfully sent MindDistracter and LifeCrusher flying several million galaxies away with a backhand slap. The fools had the gall to come bouncing into his throne room proudly declaring, "We got to the praying woman. We think she'll die."

Of course we *all* want her dead. But on *our* terms, not His. Do you remember that old Bible story about Samson? He was far weaker than this woman despite his great physical strength. Yet he did far more damage to us in his death than he ever did in his life! That thought makes me shudder. And the old woman's death could do the same thing.

Somehow the old bat must have known her time was up. Listen to this and vomit, Spitwad: "Like the gentle whisper of the wind in the pines on a starry night, my sweet Shepherd is calling me home."

She wrote that in her infernal journal. He had no right to give her that kind of advanced notice! Who does He think He is anyway?

Since she had been forewarned, she wrote down her final words in letters to each member of your host's family. It's explosive stuff, Spitwad. The moment we discovered those letters, we set loose every power available to have them lost, stolen or burned. No luck. All efforts have failed. The Adversary has them guarded like they were the Crown Jewels.

In one letter, granny passed on the family mantle of prayer to your host's little brother. That was a foolish move. We will soon have that insect eating lies from our hands like candy. He is brave and determined right now, but that courage will quickly fade once he realizes how alone he is now in the big, bad world.

Your host has practically drowned his letter with all his sentimental snifflings and slobberings. I am a bit alarmed at the depth of sorrow he is able to experience. Only a few weeks ago he would have won the school award for "most likely to end up shallow."

I warn you, Spitwad, that there is something big going on here and it has the Light written all over it. This is no amateur game we're playing here. This is the big leagues. The Adversary must be taken with deadly seriousness. It is impossible to predict exactly what He will do next, and that is what makes Him most dangerous.

The report of the withered old woman's death was both sweet and sour news. Yes, in one sense we are all breathing a sigh of relief now that she is off our backs forever. Yet there will be no party at headquarters tonight. It was all too easy. Something is up. Even Satan himself is restless. If I didn't know better I would say he's . . . afraid.

Have you read the letter to your host? I know you must have by now. That teen can read nothing else, and now her death will engrave her words even more deeply upon his soul. This Light-infested section, for example, is like a plague, a terrible disease that even now weakens your hold on him and draws him closer to the Adversary.

Dearest David,
As your name declares, you are beloved of God. This is the very God who has been my loyal

Companion, trusted Friend, guiding Shepherd, King, Lord and forgiving Savior these last 62 years. You will grieve for me when I am gone, but let your heart be at peace. I finally go to see my Lord Jesus face to face. To gaze upon His loveliness has been my longing since I was a child. You do not know Him yet, David, but He knows you.

You have tried to find happiness from the things of this world, but you have only found pain and disappointment. The heart of God aches because He knows that He alone holds the keys to real life. But you have always been a stubborn boy, wanting to try and unlock the doors on your own.

One day He will call you—a whisper in the night, perhaps, or a trumpet blast by day. But He *will* call. It will be Jesus, David. He alone is the Good Shepherd.

Beware of wolves dressed like sheep. They will also call. Yet if you truly desire the Shepherd to lead you, you will know His voice. You will know. Will you follow?

We must act quickly, Spitwad. The Adversary is on the move—but He has stupidly tipped His hand. He will soon call on your host, that much is clear. But before He does, we'll pay the frightened fool a visit. And if we play our cards right, my slow-and-sluggish apprentice, the teenage twerp will not even bother to answer the door when you-know-who comes a-knocking.

No, my friend, this ball game is far from over. We've fumbled, but now we've got the ball again. The two-minute warning has just sounded. It's crunch time and we've got to score now. And score we shall!

I have just summoned a few old teammates of mine. Their names are Guilt, Regret and Reformation. But they aren't the first team, Spitwad. There are others waiting even now for my call.

Your enraged superior,

Slimeball

The three kings bring their gifts

To most worthless Spitwad,

Now that my three honored guests have joined you, I can already sense the tide turning our way again. When you work alone, you are simply an accident waiting to happen. With help, however, you might actually come out of this whole mess looking quite good. So follow my orders exactly.

Once I explain to you how the three work together, I expect you to use some common sense and let them do their job. I absolutely forbid you to bother or nag them. No amount of whining about his being *your* host will sway me one bit. These three have had great success in the past, which is far more than I ever expect to say about you!

I wish I could have been there when my friends showed up. No doubt you were a bit alarmed by their appearances! Did you think I had asked for three of the Adversary's angels to come and punish you? The idea *had* crossed my mind . . . but anyway, the shock and surprise I'm sure you felt when the three showed up is further evidence of their brilliance.

They are masters of disguise and deception and

convincingly masquerade as angels of light. They work in the heavenly realm closest to the Light Himself, and it takes a highly trained eye like mine to discern that they are counterfeits.

They walk constantly on thin ice. They dance on the tightrope just inches away from the Adversary's camp. They climb within inches of heaven itself, following their prey as they near the point of no return. Then with wonderfully frightening swiftness, they sink their nasty claws deep into their victims, snatching them from the very jaws of the Light.

Once they have gained a foothold, they weave their web of lies and deceit, and slowly drag them back into the darkness again—to eat them at their leisure.

Guilt is really just the nickname of your first visitor. His true title is Worldly Sorrow, W.S. for short. The mental hospitals of America are the trophy cases of his work. This is how I believe he will operate.

The more your host reads granny's letter, the more he will miss her. The stage is set for Worldly Sorrow to make his grand entrance. He will most certainly begin by whispering sweet nothings into his ear like, "See how much she loved you and now she's gone. You'll never see her again. You never told her how much you cared for her, and now it's too late." And, "Can't you see how much pain you caused her by your life? Worrying about you was probably one of the main reasons she had the heart attack!"

Do you see his cunning strategy, Spitwit? Your host's crying eyes must be turned away from all that spiritual gibberish in granny's letter about the Shepherd calling. If our friend, W.S. succeeds, then the sniveling brat will begin to think far more about his relationship with that praying woman than with the Adversary.

That is our tunnel through which we can drag him back into our web of darkness.

In another part of her letter, she wrote: "David dear, I have always loved you deeply and enjoyed the times we used to spend together. Do you remember when you were a small child and I would take you to the zoo?"

This is the part of the letter that we want him to focus on. He will be overcome with sentimental feelings and pull out old pictures of himself and the old woman staring at dumb animals. How touching! W.S. will remind him, "She was just a lonely old woman with very few friends. You could have gone to see her more often, you know!"

And oh, how true, how true! He could have gone to see her more. He will not be able to deny it! Of course, he must never come to realize that she never held this fault against him.

Our kind of guilt brings us such delightful joy, because it so closely imitates the work of the Light. And the natural result of our labor is that it drowns out that dreaded voice that brings true conviction of sin.

The Adversary, if He is true to form, will try to remind your host that his stubborn self-reliance caused him only pain and disappointment. We cannot, unfortunately, completely shut out that truth. We can, however, do something quite clever to counterattack.

W.S. will paint in his mind a clear picture of a tired, lonely, deserted woman, sadly trapped in the pain of old age. Any debt that your host feels he owes toward his Creator will be swallowed up in an overwhelming sense of obligation to granny. Just perfect!

Remember, Spitwad, getting the humans to focus on pleasing people is the surest way to lure them into neglecting God. It is one of our most time-tested traps.

What they must never come to realize is that if they set their minds on pleasing God, they would automatically end up pleasing the right people!

Guilt will step in to make sure that the sympathy which wells up as a lump in your host's throat also blinds his eyes to the terrible truth about the old woman. She was not miserable at all! In fact, granny's face literally beamed with the joy of the Light! I had to wear sunglasses just to bring myself to look at her.

It's amazing how his guilty conscience will deepen the wrinkles, hollow out the cheeks, and sadden the eyes of granny as he pictures her in his mind.

Your host's mother, fighting her personal battles with guilt, will try to ease her own accusing conscience as she tries to soothe her son's. She'll say stupid things like, "Please dear, there's no sense in punishing yourself now. You can't change the past. What's done is done." She will try to give him a reassuring hug, but he will pull away, more certain than ever that he has been a total jerk. We couldn't agree more.

So, enter visitor number two—Regret.

Regret's job is to act as a kind of bridge over troubled

waters. You see, my clueless Spitwad, we cannot count on your host's guilty grief to last very long. He's a teenager with an attention span about as predictable as a hurricane. The flowers will fade on granny's grave and the false guilt will fade in your host's heart. And once those helpful emotions are gone, it will be far more difficult to fog up his thinking. He will again be vulnerable to the Adversary's conviction.

In case you hadn't noticed the difference, Spitwad, here it is: *Worldly Sorrow* drives people away from God (just check out Adam and Eve in the Garden). *Godly sorrow*, the Light's conviction, moves people toward God. That's why he must never be allowed to experience *that*.

We must beat the Heavenly Troublemaker to the punch. And this is where Regret comes in. One wrong move at this point and our victim could fall off the bridge and plunge into the swift current of the Adversary's River of Repentance. He would then wash up on the Shores of Salvation and be lost forever. He *must* cross this bridge safely—and that is Regret's job.

There is a small yet incredibly important difference between regret and repentance. But the end results are anything but similar!

Do you remember the stories about Peter and Judas from that hateful Book? Remember Judas? He is Regret's prize catch. He can still be heard down here muttering over and over to himself, "He was an innocent man . . ."

You see, Judas betrayed the Crucified One and

killed himself out of regret. But Peter denied Him and died to himself in repentance. And remember what he did to us with his hated preaching! ...

You see, Spitwad, *Regret* will move your host to say to himself, "If only I had not been so selfish, this probably would not have happened. I should have been more sensitive. I have been so self-centered, I could just kick myself!"

Repentance (may it never happen in our lifetime!) would move him to say, "Oh Jesus (I can barely spit that name out!), I have lived my whole life for myself; I see that it is wrong. Your way is right."

Do you see the difference? It is the difference between death and life! We don't mind if your unhappy host ends up turning over a new leaf, as long as he doesn't discover the Light under it.

It would be nice, of course, if he would simply go out and hang his teenage carcass from a tree like Judas, the man who betrayed Jesus, did. Then he would be out of the Adversary's clutches forever. Unfortunately, his guilt is not that kind.

Like Judas, however, he *does* believe that he has betrayed an innocent person ... granny. And like Judas, we must make sure he bypasses the forgiveness that the Innocent One offers. If that happens, he has crossed the bridge of regret safely.

Then we can escort our prey deeper and deeper into the tunnel, and through to the other side into the bright, optimistic and hopeful land of Reformation. Reformation just happens to be visitor number three.

Don't you find Reformation a little hard to take—upbeat, confident, determined, optimistic, proud and (I use the term tongue-in-cheek) . . . *good?*

His mission is to start your host on a whole program of self-improvement. It will be kind of like a whole set of New Year's resolutions, only this time the teen will be dead serious about it.

Remember, these resolutions will not be born of an empty holiday tradition, with a drink in one hand, crossed fingers on the other. His new path of life will come from a soul devilishly dipped in deep, generous portions of Worldly Sorrow and Regret.

The fool really wants to become a better person . . . for his grandmother. And that is the beauty of the plan. He is determined to become the man granny always wished he'd become—with one key piece of the puzzle left out . . . the Light Himself. "There is a way which seems right to a man, but its end is the way of death."[1] Let's make sure Davey boy follows that path!

After he sweats and struggles for a while along the hot, dusty road of self-improvement, his mental picture of granny will change. Now he sees a sad, lonely face. In time, she will become a hard-driving, never-satisfied, wrinkle-faced slave driver. And that will be a fitting end to that praying woman.

Until that happens, Spitwad, it would be a good idea to find a way to have your host misplace granny's letter. There are too many unpleasant reminders in it.

---

1 Proverbs 14:12

The Adversary will not guard it forever, so watch for your chance.

Oh, by the way, you need not worry about any prayer attacks coming by way of your host's little brother. The traitor has already found a new thing to occupy his time and energy.

He has made the All-Star soccer team. And, thanks to the efforts of TimeWaster, the coach is demanding a heavy load of practices and travel for the rug rats.

Even now his foolish dreams of being a great prayer warrior are being replaced with daydreams about being a sports star. Oh poor, poor fallen star.

I knew he could be handled with ease. Even now he doesn't remember to pray for your host very often. In fact, the prayer protection over the whole family is almost gone. I feel it is nearly time to close in for the kill. The first team will soon be joining you.

Your superior optimist,

Slimeball

Send in the varsity squad!

To most unworthy Spitwad,

Now that over a year has gone by since your new assignment in Suburbia, USA, it is high time for an evaluation. Is your host closer to becoming one with us than when you began with him? Well, thanks to the work of the "three kings" that I sent you, I say that the answer is yes. That trio brought very precious gifts for your child, and he is progressing quite well. No thanks to you, I might add.

I must admit, after reading your report of the past few months, that I felt just like I do when a good gang war breaks out—fully satisfied. It appears that your host has been fully duped and doped with the driving thought that he "failed Granny."

That's fine as far as it goes. But it doesn't go far enough. It would be wise to begin suggesting to him that he has also failed *himself*. Improving himself for granny's sake is already wearing thin, just as we expected. Improving himself for himself is an addiction that could last for a lifetime—or an eternity!

Let it never, never occur to him (except in the most vague sort of way) that he has failed our Adversary. It's okay and even somewhat helpful for him to think things like: "Well, God certainly understands my mistakes and doesn't expect me to be perfect!"

And that becomes even more useful when he follows that line of thinking with: "Besides, I'm a much better person than _____." He will fill in the blank.

The Light's way is to justify a person by his trust in the Crucified and Risen One. Our way is to get people to justify themselves by comparison with other people.

Need I caution you, Snot-nose, that as long as he compares himself to his teenage buddies, he'll be fairly safe. Unless he starts stacking his life up against Steve's, that is. But if he ever compares himself to the Hated Risen One, he is (and we are) in deep doo-doo. Our Adversary will see to that.

Encourage him to view his failures in terms like, "I should've known better. I won't make *that* mistake again." That will keep him right where we want him.

Given enough time, your host could become a strong candidate for "Humanist of the Year." Do you remember that old saying of ours: "Every day in every way, I just keep getting better and better." The fool believes it now. All is going precisely according to plan.

The marvelous thing to watch, my blind apprentice, is that in many ways his self-improvement plan *is* working. The lad is actually becoming more decent, considerate and understanding . . . at least on the outside. He tries hard to listen and understand people. He even visits nursing homes! If he were actually in the Enemy's camp, he would be downright nauseating.

Even his parents have noticed the difference. They regard him as more responsible and mature. He does his chores around the house without complaining and he even stays home a bit more at night and on the weekends.

Overall, it's all quite delicious, don't you think? I can now pronounce with confidence that we are inside the Adversary's 20-yard line, my anxious pupil. And it's first down and ten.

The first team is about to enter the game. They have already been warming up. Their names? Pride and Self-Righteousness. They will score. They always do. The game is nearly ours!

Back to the game plan. Your host is feeling pretty good about himself these days, as well he should. He is the ultimate boy scout, junior achiever and teacher's pet all rolled into one.

And he's about to ride his high horse straight into the palm of our hand.

As you will see, Pride and Self-Righteousness work together, at the same time. They are really a rather irritating pair, but this dynamic duo knows what they are doing. No question about it.

Since they travel around like Siamese twins (joined at the heart), each one a shadow of the other, let me clue you in on how to tell them apart. Look at their eyes. Pride's eyes are always focused on himself—his own beauty, power, intelligence, goodness, accomplishments, etc.

The eyes of Self-Righteousness, however, are constantly on the move, looking around, comparing himself to others. And he has two very small but powerful creatures perched on his eyebrows. They are Judgment and Critical Spirit. They go with him everywhere, making sure your host focuses on the faults of others. In this way, your boy will always be sure to feel good about himself.

The whole area of self-esteem is a half-truth that we have blown way out of proportion. You see, Spitwad, when it comes to self-esteem there are really only two kinds of people in the world. There are those who feel good about themselves and those who feel bad about themselves.

Some of those in the first group feel good about themselves because they have fallen into the Light's grasp. They have strong self-esteem because they are God's "precious" children, foolishly accepted and loved by Him. This is the most dangerous group.

A second group is where your host is now. He has what appears to be a healthy self-image because he is confident, optimistic and happy. But the foundation for his self-love is sinking sand. His mansion of comfortable living is actually a house of cards that is doomed to fall, for it is based on deception. He is still a wicked sinner at heart; but don't try to tell him that! He is too puffed up to see his fatal flaws now anyway. So for the time being he lives in blissful ignorance.

The next group of people consists of the ones who are under the Adversary's conviction process. He is stripping away all their facades and their eyes are being opened to their wretched (so He says!) sinfulness. They are perched right outside the doorway to the House of Salvation and represent a spiritual emergency, requiring urgent action. The Light is getting through to them. Your host must never reach this point.

The last group are those numerous humans (both Christian and non-Christian) who are wonderfully wallowing in the slime of our accusations and condemnations. They feel too weak to climb up out of the muck and too worthless to ask for help. They are our favorites to bully around. They feel bad because *we* are getting through to them!

But back to Pride and Self-Righteousness. Already your host has welcomed the two visitors and has begun to see himself and the world through their eyes. Notice how the smile that used to genuinely cross his face upon leaving the nursing homes has now become a smirk? He's not thinking about the old people when he leaves; he's thinking about how good all this community service stuff will look on his résumé. And how impressed the university admissions people will be.

And do you think it is with compassion that he now views his schoolmates? Was that not just the faintest glimmer of conceited superiority on his face after he counseled one of his friends?

Yes indeed, after many months of work, the success of his self-improvement program has become evident to all. Many greatly admire him and seek out his advice. But not all of them. Some of his old friends are now jealous and resent him.

Strange isn't it, how easily the proud teen slithered from being a caring counselor to a wise advisor to Brother Superior. The shift was gradual and barely noticeable to most people. Of course, now one practically has to set up an appointment months in advance just to talk to the cocky little twerp.

His closer friends, Steve included of course, can already sense the proud change in him and they are worried. Your host will become more and more blind and deaf to their concerns as long as our Siamese twins hang around. He is too busy right now having the time of his empty life. Let him enjoy!

His equally blind classmates are so captivated by his changed life that they're talking about nominating him for senior class president next year. *Only we could pull off a stunt like that.* From geek to god in a year . . . while his heart goes farther and farther into our deep freeze!

Things will eventually turn sour for him, you know. Disneyland won't last forever. One day the teenage bag of hot air will wake up to find his appointment calendar empty.

Even now, if you look closely, you can see other forces at work in him. He figures he has already more than paid off his debt to granny. In fact, he rarely thinks of her anymore. He is even beginning, deep down, to find the whole goody-two-shoes game to be a bit of a bore.

And that is where we must drive home one of our most potent wedges between the puppet and his Heavenly Puppeteer. It is time for Pinocchio to become a real man and break free of the controlling strings of his Heavenly Gepetto.

For that to happen, your host must become convinced that being good and having fun simply cannot happen at the same time.

The longer he works at trying to help people, the more drained he will become. Any fun he still has will come from the ego trip of "being needed." That will wear thin very fast once he realizes how demanding people can be on his time and energy. He will then be faced with a choice—help people and have no free time for himself or have fun and forget the rest of the world. The choice will come easily for him.

It's a cruel game we play, eh Spitwad? Throwing sticks for the dogs to fetch? Ah, cruel indeed, but not a game at all. Ever since our Most Clever Master deceived the original woman in the Garden (tricking her into doubting God's goodness and love), we have been about the deadly serious business of driving a wedge between the Creator and His creatures.

If we play our cards right, we can pound the stake of discontent deep into your host's heart.

We will fill his mind with thoughts like: "God wants me to be good. Being good is hard work and not a lot of fun. Having fun is necessary in order for me to be happy. Being good and following God are going to take away my happiness. But I want to be happy. Therefore, I will not follow God." Simple? Oh yes. But powerful and effective, too, as millions of tormented souls down here will admit.

So what lies in store for your host? It is time to let nature takes its course. He has had to hold back his natural urges too long. For months he has worked hard at trying to be a good boy. The pendulum is about to swing back again. After all, he *is* still a gland-gorged, hormone-hungry teen.

In due time we may want to get him and the blond bimbo back together. I understand that she is on the prowl again. I trust that your host will be also. His pride will get excited about the idea of conquering her—and his lust will second that emotion.

We had to push hard to get the lad to swing on the pendulum toward being good. He should find the return ride back into darkness to be quite refreshing and easy.

And this has been my plan all along, Spitwad.

Your strategic superior,

Slimeball

The religious cafeteria

I was happy to hear that your host has been hanging out more at church lately. At Bilgewater's church, that is. It has become an important part of his recent self-improvement kick.

That church is filled to the brim with people who consider themselves to be religious, good people. Many of them are convinced, as is your host, that they are God's gift to the world. They go around trying to help people (whether their victims want help or not), growing more and more proud of themselves with each deed they do.

The lad is convinced that the church youth group desperately needs his presence. Now *why* that group exists at all is somewhat of a mystery. It probably was started because someone came to the conclusion that every church needs a youth group. It keeps the teenagers who swarm there out of their parents' hair for an hour each week, if nothing else.

Anyway, if the truth be known, most of the 13- to 18-year-old crowd who attend Sunday morning services would not be caught dead at the youth group. The image of the group by those who are cool is that it is sort of a halfway house for lonely nerds. Most of the kids view the youth group leaders as being hopelessly out of touch with reality.

That is exactly what we desire. Once a teen begins to view church as old and boring, it is only a matter of time before they see our Adversary the same way.

You asked the question as to whether you should permit your host to talk to the various religious door-to-door salespeople who regularly make the subdivision rounds.

Of course it's all right, you nitwit! As long as they are on our team and not on the Light's, the more the merrier! Confusion is one of our most potent weapons!

Since you have been out of the country for quite a while (and out of your mind for much longer), I guess I'll have to refresh your memory a bit.

Spudwhip, don't even try to keep track of all the different religions, cults, sects, and philosophies that are out there. Even I lose track of one or two.

After all, it's hard enough keeping track of millions of Hindus and their numerous sects of varied shapes, sizes and colors, not to mention the small groups. Did you ever hear of the "Jesus, the Mushroom" cult? It had one member; I understand he was a real *fun guy!*

Of course, all of them were started with a little help from our friends. And our menu of false religions has delicious items for people of all different tastes.

The Light is so narrow, making everyone eat the same food! We are far more in touch with the personal preferences of our customers.

To the nasty, angry, over-patriotic types we offer fundamentalist Islam, Nazism, the Ku Klux Klan (which is Nazism American-style), and those weirdo cults that hang out in the hills stockpiling guns and waiting for the return of Christ. David Koresh was one of our most devoted customers.

To those who are more mystical, we provide a whole buffet of Oriental foods, such as Buddhism, Taoism, Confucianism (for the confused) and Hinduism. One can sample several of these at once or order additional items from the New Age a la carte menu.

For those people who want more of a sense of *community* and *cause*, we heartily recommend the Unification Church (AKA the Moonies), Krishna Consciousness (whose followers' brains are unconscious), Mormonism or Jehovah's Witnesses. The last two are especially appealing to those who want to stay closest to the Adversary's camp while still being in ours.

Of course, there are thousands more to choose from, and we encourage the "religious seeker" to taste each dish for a while before sampling another. In that way, one can lead one's host down the primrose path of false religions until the day he drops dead.

Your host is far too middle-class, suburban America to fly eastern. But one day he may be perfect prey for the Latter-day Saints or Watchtower vultures. They are about as middle-class suburbia as you can get (next to the Masons, that is).

For those who have always wanted to start their own "business," we offer full religious franchise ownerships.

Kind of like owning your very own fast religious-food restaurant. Cult leaders stand to gain a fine, fine income if successful, and we'll give them all the help they need. With no strings attached . . . only chains! I guess you could say, Spitwad, that we'll help them open a whole *chain* of "restaurants." Get it? *Chain* of restaurants. Oh forget it.

Joseph Smith, Charles Taze Russell, Mohammed, Gautama, you name them, they're all here. And all highly successful they were! A *sizzling* success, you might say. Eh, Spitwad?

You may be wondering (though most likely you are not, since the act of *wondering* indicates a brain that is actually working) why *Religiosity* (being religious) flows so smoothly in the wake of the "good ships" *Pride* and *Self-Righteousness*. Perhaps this "domino effect" can be stated simply enough for even you to grasp.

Pride says, "I am great (or good or smart or capable or beautiful or whatever) and I alone deserve the credit for that. I recognize this is obvious and so should you."

Self-Righteousness says, "I am holier than you. I am, therefore, a better person than you."

Religiosity says, "I work hard at pleasing God, harder than most. I recognize that and so does God. Therefore, God *is* pleased with me. I, therefore, will worship God and help my fellow man."

I know, I know, Spitwad, break out the Pepto Dismal. Religious people *are* some of the most nauseating humans around. But they provide some amusing entertainment at times.

The most disgusting kind are those I call the *Religiously Insecure*. They show up at church every chance they get, hoping against hope that they will finally do enough to truly please God. They are like dogs who crawl on their bellies before their master, hoping for just one little pat on their heads and a "Good boy!"

I don't have time to chitchat about this matter. You will run into all the different religious breeds over time. For example, there are the *Denominational Bigot* or his cousin, the *Doctrinally Pure Pharisee*, the *Ecumenical Wimp,* the *Religious Experience Junkie* and the *Country Club Social Butterfly.* My favorite is the one who comes to church every Sunday but never gets involved and never changes. He's called the *Pleasingly Plump Pew Potato.*

Anyway, it's enough to realize that your host is unlikely to last long in his current religious fling. He is starting to feel uneasy in the role—mostly because there aren't any cute girls in his youth group!

So be encouraged. Even though the winter chill of his religious pride is beginning to thaw, the warm, sensual winds of spring are blowing again inside of him.

And you know what comes after spring, don't you, Spitwad? That's right, the red-hot, simmering summer. And after the summer? Why, the fall, of course. And everyone knows that pride goes before the fall. May it be so.

Your religious superior,

Slimeball

Disturbing developments:
Good, Bad and Ugly

To most unworthy Spitwad,

As of right now I am officially placing you on Stage Four Alert, Spitwad. Let me spell out for you what is happening and then draw some crucial observations. It is obvious you would never have pieced this together yourself.

If you look at each of these things separately you might miss their significance. They might seem to be merely the normal day-in-and-day-out routine of these pathetic humans. I must quickly add, my naive knucklehead, that the Light has done some of His most terrible work hidden in the seemingly innocent cloak of the everyday. The list is as follows:

1. That bimbo blond has set her sights on the football jerk, Light-lover, Steve.

2. This jock friend of your host's continues to bug him about coming to the youth group with him.

3. Your host, despite his current superiority complex and numerous duties at his church, is growing more curious about what goes on at Steve's

church (teen translation: He wants to check out the babes there).

4. Your host is thinking again of what it would be like to go to bed with the blond.

5. Next month, the Adversary's Lighthouse has scheduled a large youth rally with a well-known Christian rock band. The speaker, a noted enemy of ours, will present a talk called "Sex: Why Not?"

Spitwad, the present target of the floozy has no interest in her (except in some of the dreams GuiltMerchant creates in his mind), but she does not give up easily. She has invited herself to join his group of Light-lovers as they attend the rally.

Your host, no doubt, will be invited to join that same group. He will want to attend, once he hears that the message will be about sex and that she will be there, too.

He must not, I repeat, must not be permitted to go! Have I made myself perfectly clear?

How do I suggest you stop him from going? I suggest that you try and work through your host's parents, raising some red flags in their minds about his becoming too much of a religious fanatic. Create in mommy's head the image of people in that "other church" lifting their hands, shouting amen and hallelujah, falling in the aisles, speaking in tongues, etc. A few "frothing at the mouth" and "rolling of the eyes" images will do nicely, too.

Whatever it takes to create the religious horror film in her mind will pay off, believe me.

One more thing of interest on the homefront. You should know that your host's little brother is doing quite well on his All-Star soccer team. It takes up quite a bit of his time and energy and occupies most of his waking thoughts. *This is good.*

He has also made some new friends on the team. His best new friend just happens to be the younger brother of the blond's current football flame. That's right, Spitwad, he is Steve's younger brother. And he also happens to be a very committed Light-lover. *This is bad.*

And I thought you'd be interested in knowing that your host's soccer-playing pest of a brother picked up his Bible for the first time in many weeks today. And there were tears in his eyes as he read. *This is ugly.*

Your alert superior,

Slimeball

Post-rally mop up operation

To most lucky but still worthless Spitwad,

The account of what happened at the youth rally reads like the plot of some grade-B horror movie! It has already been dubbed down here, "The Invasion of the Soul Snatcher."

Never before have I witnessed such a mess. This place is like a beehive on fire with all the tormentors, imps, tempters, fiends and torturers flying in and out of here. It's O'Hairy Airport, and everything is in chaos . . . except for me, of course. *Somebody* has to keep his wits about him.

One can hardly hear himself think down here with all the pleadings, whines, and blubbering excuses coming from the newly arrived horde of now homeless demons.

Soon, however, I hope things will calm down to normal and all we'll hear are the shrieks, moans, wails and groans as the torturers do what they do best. You are lucky, Spitwad, to be spared this time.

The fact that you are there and not here is utterly amazing to me, in light of your track record. You were, it seems, able to prevent your host from attending the rally. I hate to admit it, but your crude idea turned out to be effective.

The invitation from your host's coach to take him and some other players to the pro basketball playoff game was an offer he simply could not refuse. He *wanted* to refuse it because his flesh was focused fully on the girl, but he also saw his chance to win brownie points with the coach.

And so, reasoning that he would have other shots at her, he took the bait and made the politically correct choice to go to the game.

Your trembling request to Eclipse that tickets right behind the home bench somehow find their way from a certain Leaven member to the coach was risky. But Eclipse liked the idea and it worked.

But, my dear Spitwad, your host made one serious mistake in his judgment of the blond. He failed to anticipate the working of the Light. That is always a fatal error. Yes, oh ignorant and blind fool that you are, she (like scores of other teenage traitors) was seduced by the Adversary at the rally! She is gone.

And what a horrible scene it was! The whole wretched place was like a laser light show with thousands of angelic goons shooting around the auditorium like rockets. Our defenses were shredded like that dry and tasteless wheat cereal those mortals eat for breakfast. Countless demon-hours of labor withered under the assault.

And then the Quiet One manifested Himself. Yes, Spitwad, the Spirit of God Himself showed up, descending upon that room like a blanket of searing, blinding lightning.

Most of our heroic forces panicked and scurried for cover, deserting their hosts in their hour of greatest need. It was a massacre, plain and simple. And now, of course, yours truly must somehow try to pick up the pieces from it all. Oh well, at times it is such a burden being needed as much as I am.

There were, however, a few of our fine-feathered fiends who had the guts to stick around long enough to water down the Adversary's gospel in the minds of some of our victims.

The deceiving spirits were able to cause such an excitement about "letting Jesus into your life" (which is absolutely the most revolting of all possessions!) that the call to repent of your sins was missed by many. That resulted in a number of spiritual miscarriages— people thinking they had been born again when they had really not!

Those kind of purely emotional "decisions for Christ" tend to sputter and fizzle out quickly. Then, once they have given up on God, we can send them out as *our* evangelists preaching the good news that, "Yeah, I tried that Jesus stuff once, but it didn't work. It was all a bunch of hype and mind control." Before long, they can be convinced that they escaped by the skin of their teeth from some sneaky religious cult.

You see, it is those who have tasted the watered-down gospel and then spit it out who are some of the toughest to convert to the real thing in the future. They are like people who have received a vaccine against a disease. The shot in their arm is a mild form of the disease which protects them against the real thing.

For now, they are excited about their new faith. It is kind of the in thing to talk about at school, since so many of the cool kids were there. But I'm not worried. Once those spiritual duds stop their happy popping and crackling, they will become some of our most effective promoters.

No, Spitwad, the ones who were *truly* kidnapped into the camp of the Light are the ones that concern me. And that includes the traitorous blond.

The queen of lust herself has now taken the vow of chastity. And I dare say, half the male population of the high school is now in a state of shock . . . and mourning. Your host is no exception.

Needless to say, your poor puppy's pea brain is reeling with the question: "What in the world could be so great about religion to make someone give up sex?" That's exactly the question I have. And remember, your host knows religion. And he thinks he knows sex.

Well, exactly how long she will be able to play the role of high school nun remains to be seen. But for now, Sister Blond is ablaze with the Adversary's fire. And this is the real thing, baby. Do not underestimate the damage that brazen little vixen can do if she truly becomes energized by the Light.

And make no mistake about it. The Adversary is shameless in these things. He will use her as long as possible to further His cause.

Spitwad, listen to me. Our backs are against the

wall. The little she-traitor is already praying for your host and has plans to talk with him. He will be delighted at the chance just to be in the presence of her body, his curiosity and lust are already aroused.

I have already made an urgent request that this meeting be stopped. It is a clear violation and trespass on our territory. He belongs to us by his own permission.

As usual, my pleas have fallen on deaf ears. The objection was overruled by the Judge. He is guilty of the most obvious conflicts of interest in these matters. It's just not fair! The meeting *will* take place.

Your job is to convince your host that he is *already* a Christian. A timely phone call from Bilgewater to remind him of his baptism and confirmation couldn't hurt.

Help him to see that the blond's excited rantings and ravings about his need to be "born again" and "saved" are funny and totally uncool. Whisper words like *fundamentalist* and *Bible-banger* into his mind when she preaches to him.

Make sure a rather smug and superior smirk crosses his face as she witnesses to him. This will make her angry and she will quickly lose touch with the Light's assistance and power. Then our defenses may be able to hold.

Don't forget to remind your host continually that he is a member in good standing of the oldest, most well-established church in town. (Of course, *we* know that it is also the deadest church in town!) And don't let him forget that recently his attendance and service record have been exemplary.

If you are clever (a tall order, I realize), you can even cause the thought to pop into his brain that she is getting an awful lot of attention around school for such a recent, flash-in-the-pan change of heart. After all, *he* has been living a good, moral life for quite a while now. A lot longer than she has, that's for sure. Encourage him to think, "*I* should be the one talking to *her* about God! Who does she think she is anyway?"

Do you remember the older brother in the Risen One's parable of the prodigal son? (It's in Luke 15 if you're wondering.) The older brother was irritated with the father when his brother came home after living in sin and the dad threw a party for him. His resentment toward his brother makes for very pleasant reading. Let the "spirit of the older brother" live on in your host and you will do well.

One warning, however. Your host still longs for this wench's body. He may decide to pretend he is actually interested in her spiritual hogwash in order to try and score with her.

This strategy, should he attempt it, will only succeed in prolonging her preaching! It will not succeed in winning her. She does not want him. Her eyes are still locked on Steve. And now that she is a fellow Light-lover, his interest in her has awakened. They are both the foulest garbage. They deserve each other.

Spitwad, you are now officially on Stage Five Alert. Full Alert. Your host is very vulnerable right now, despite all of my brave efforts. A full blown invasion by the Adversary has already begun and an attack on your host is imminent.

The Adversary's Lighthouse has groups of prayer pests popping up like pimples everywhere. We have, however, already begun to develop a strategy that will punish them severely for this.

But for now, they pray with great energy and frightening power. And the Adversary inclines His ear to them.

As for your host's little brother, have you noticed that he has taken to the practice of reading the Bible while on his knees? His soccer friend taught him that. Isn't that sweet? I hate them all and have had enough of children meddling in our plans. Both of them will one day pay dearly for interfering in the affairs of such high majesties and powers as ours.

Could you have ever imagined it possible—to be stopped by a bunch of snot-nosed kids?

We *will* bring this town back under our yoke, Spitwad. And mark my words: Our yoke will not be easy.

> Your superior with
> a superior migraine,
>
> Slimeball

A security leak

To most worthless Spitwad,

I had not planned on sending this to you today, but something has come up which complicates matters significantly. And we can ill-afford any more heat from the fires below!

I will get right to the point. Leaven has been discovered. The two teenage Light-lovers (the bimbo and the jock-jerk) were driving back home from a date downtown. They decided to bypass some of the traffic lights on the main highway and chose to use an old, lightly-traveled back road that winds through a heavily wooded area.

As they rounded a curve, they spotted taillights of a car turning down an overgrown dirt road. Thinking it might be some of their high school friends looking for a secret place to make out, they waited a few minutes and then followed.

You know what they found—a padlocked gate in a rusted fence blocking the way of any unwelcome vehicle. Thinking that they must have stumbled upon someone's private residence, Steve was satisfied and prepared to go home. Besides, he said to her, he was starting to feel the creeps out there in the middle of nowhere. Speaking of "creeps," you weren't there, were you, Spitwad?

As bad luck would have it, the girl's curiosity was far too aroused to go back. She was determined to go on in and have a look around, whether her date wanted to or not. Of course he gave in (feeling the obligation to protect her and not wanting to appear to be chicken!) and so they climbed over the fence and hiked inside.

Our spirit guards were watching the whole scene and heard it all.

You were stumbling around in the jungles of Thailand at the time, but a couple years ago I protested as strong as I dared when Leaven chose this location. When Eclipse announced he was going to use an abandoned house in my district for the meeting place of the local coven of Leaven, I threatened to resign. They just laughed at me and tried to convince me that it was an honor to be chosen.

An honor, humph! It has been more like having a live artillery shell in your back yard, Spitwad! Every moment of every day I worried about the moment when the blasted thing would go off. And now it has! And guess who will be accused of gross negligence? Me! It is a curse, I tell you. A curse!

The two fools set foot where angels fear to tread, and now they pose a serious security threat. They peered through a crack in the wall of the abandoned house, and saw enough to know what was going on. Fortunately, they could see no faces, but they were able to memorize the numbers of three of the license plates from the 12 cars parked outside.

A potentially very damaging bit of evidence if followed up by the wrong party, wouldn't you say, Spitwad? Do you realize who was at that meeting? A very influential university president. An outspoken talk show host. The mayor. And so on. The teen troublemakers would have memorized all the numbers if the jock hadn't gotten spooked. He literally had to drag the blond out of there.

All their spying might have gone undetected by the Leavenites if the thirteenth member of the coven had not been delayed by an accident on the freeway. His detour cost him precious time, but may have saved all their precious necks. He had the presence of mind to write down the license plate number of the jock's car and then drive a safe distance away and wait until they drove off.

Our unseen agents overheard the two meddlers discussing their strategy as they drove home. They decided that they would not tell anyone what they saw, and just go see the city police chief first thing in the morning.

Smart move. I just hope they don't make it *too* early. After all, that will be Saturday morning and the police chief is likely to be quite tired out from a hard week of work. Plus he also happened to be attending a very important meeting that lasted well after midnight . . . a meeting in an old, abandoned house somewhere in the deep woods outside of town.

The police chief will be ready for his two teenage visitors in the morning.

Your nervous superior,

Slimeball

Your host becomes your enemy

To utterly and completely worthless Spitwad,

Your appointment with the torturers is set for two weeks from this coming Tuesday. Luckily for you there is a heavy backlog of cases left over from that awful youth rally, or you'd already be smarting from your caning.

May I strongly suggest that you not make any plans for the weeks immediately following your therapy. In fact, it would be a terrific time to take your two weeks of vacation. And while you're at it, why don't you do us all a big favor and take two years of vacation!

I'm just sick and tired of you, Sputterweed. I'm already long overdue for a vacation from you and all your crying and whining.

It is only with a great deal of effort that I am able to restrain my fury at your pitiful performance these past few weeks. But one can only yell and scream for so long, and then one must deal with reality once again. You have heard my threats. You have felt the hot breath of my rage. And now you will listen to my rebuke. I hope your scales blister and fall off, you imbecile!

If your case had not been just one of scores of defeats

in my principality during the last several months, you would certainly have joined HeartFreezer by now. I want you to know that I pushed for that punishment immediately. Ah, to have you banished forever . . . so near and yet so far.

Part of what saved your scaly skin is that compared to the others who caved in so quickly at the rally, you look rather good. But I know better. The mere mention of your name makes me start to twitch uncontrollably. I have developed a very irritating nervous condition of late, and it is clearly all your fault.

But, as cruel fate would have it, my superiors insist on keeping me in the role of your caretaker and trainer. Babysitter is more like it. No doubt I am the victim of some back-room politics by BloodCraver and perhaps by Molech himself. They have had it in for me ever since that Christian Crisis Pregnancy Center opened up in town. They blame me for that, of course, saying I am responsible for robbing them of some of their food.

Perhaps I should not have suggested to BloodCraver that he try the local Red Cross blood bank if he was so desperate. Those Type-A personalities simply have no sense of humor at all.

Anyway, Nitwit, I have listened to your usual squealings that "It wasn't my fault!" You had expected the blond girl to be an emotional, easily-flustered flop of an evangelist, didn't you? Where in the world did you ever get that idea?

You were caught completely off-guard when she

attended the evangelism training seminar at the Light-house. You should be ashamed.

I know that most churches do not bother to train their new converts in personal witnessing right away. They keep them untrained during those early days of youthful spiritual zeal and enthusiasm for the Adversary. That's to our benefit.

So generally new Light-lovers come on too strong and end up turning off all their friends. Or they separate themselves completely from them so as not to be polluted by their sin.

That's the way we wish it always would be—new lamps hidden under the basket instead of shining the Light everywhere.

Well, Spitdrip, you were fooled again. One of those parachurch groups linked up with the Lighthouse to provide evangelism training for new members. I swear those Light-infested troublemakers would storm the gates of hell with a water pistol!

The tramp went to the training. She tried out the training on your host. And now she's hooked forever, because your host swallowed the bait.

If I have to hear one more heavenly outburst of Hallelujah! coming from those obnoxious angels, I'm going to have a complete nervous breakdown. Naturally, I suspected all along that you would be no match for the Light. It was only a matter of time before your true yellow color showed up.

"What could I have done?" you plead. Oh my badness, Clodwad, have you gone completely brain dead?

When the girl started yacking about the Adversary's love, you could have brought up any number of effective diversions. But no! You froze up when she drew the sword of John 3:16. Now don't tell me you've forgotten John 3:16? You Jello-head! "For God so loved the world, that He gave His only begotten Son, that whoever believes in Him should not perish, but have eternal life." That is the most hated verse from that hideous Book! I should stew you in your slimy green juices for making me quote it.

You could have easily deflected that sword attack by reminding your host that he had memorized that verse as a child—that it was nothing new. You jerk, don't you remember that when the "good news" becomes "old news," that usually means good news for us?

Why didn't you have him argue against the idea of a loving God by bringing up the question of why there is so much evil and suffering in the world? He could then have stood up and ended the conversation right there saying, "I'm sorry, but I cannot put my trust in such a cold, uncaring God." And that would have been the end of it. She could not have handled that situation.

What were you doing when she plunged on ahead and started preaching about sin? Were you listening to her, too? Were you thinking of turning to the Light like your host?

Wouldn't that have been just great. I would have been the laughingstock of all hell, going down in the history books as having trained the first demon ever converted to Christianity!

You fool! Why do you fear the Enemy's sword so much but do not tremble before the power of the torturers? You will not make that mistake again, I guarantee that!

Of all the places where your host could have been encouraged to resist the foul odor of the gospel, it should have been in the matter of his sinfulness. Your host easily could have been prompted to speak of his many church-related acts of service and devotion to God. She might even have been tempted to ask the question, "Are you a Christian, David?" too soon. He would have quickly assured her that he was, thus sparing us the agony later on when he found out that he was not!

And why didn't you have him remind the floozy of her colorful past? You could have sown a seed of doubt in her mind regarding her worthiness to talk with your now-religious host.

But then came the part about the cross! Oh that cursed, cursed cross! How I cringe in horror as I recall the face of the Crucified One. That joyful agony. That horrified hope! His tortured tranquillity!

Two thousand years ago, victory was ours—or so it seemed. Then all at once it was torn from our grasp as He uttered that final, "triumphant" cry, "It is finished!" We all howled in rage and terror when we realized we had been tricked—fatally deceived by the Adversary! We were beaten at our own game. Lured into being destroyed by our own weapon, death! By nailing Him to that tree, we were actually nailing ourselves inside our own coffins!

How could you have not stopped the whole conversation, Zitwit, when the girl began to speak of that hated resurrection. I can barely bring myself to say that word, somehow its power controls me even now . . .

By that time, you mindless coward, I imagine you had lost all presence of mind and had fled the scene of your defeat. Shortly after that, your host fell under the spell of the Quiet One, and he too was gone. Forever.

The monument to himself that your host had built from his own good works crumbled under the conviction of his sin. He saw that the monument was really an altar to worship himself. Even the crust that we had so skillfully formed around his proud, cold heart cracked and fell away. Like a jack-hammer, the Light's insane love for him blasted it all away.

The ice melted and he went crawling like the rest of them to the invitation of grace, forgiveness and unconditional acceptance in Christ.

Oh yes, the invitation is supposedly a free gift—but there is a cost. He has lost forever the supreme joy and freedom that comes from serving himself. He will soon see that he had it much, much easier when he was with us.

Have we lost? No way. As far as I am concerned, Spitwad, the war has just begun. Yes, we have lost the fight for your host's miserable soul, due largely to your typical bungling. But there are many more battles yet to be fought . . . and won.

Before he made the fatal decision, he was your host. Now he has become your mortal enemy.

Your sick and tired superior,

Slimeball

Starting over

To most useless Spitwad,

True, it is the greatest of all victories to escort one of our Adversary's precious human specimens into our eternal home in hell. But there are other pleasures.

We lost one battle, but there is still work to do! Time to get busy. Even though we lost your host, we can still get to him. It is sheer ecstasy to torment the Light's redeemed children, making them feel worthless, unloved, unwanted and hopeless. But an even greater pleasure is to use one of His bratty kids for *our* purposes.

Such a high calling as this I picture for your ex-host. I shall, from now on, refer to him as *your enemy*, for that is what he is.

Our Adversary has stupidly chosen to show mercy to your enemy's wicked soul. We shall torment it unmercifully. The Light has poured out His love on him. We shall drown the traitor in our hate. Your enemy has foolishly rejected us and chosen life. We shall make him wish he were dead.

There is one piece of good news in the midst of all these terrible conversions. At their meeting, the police chief assured the two teenage snoops that the department was fully aware of the activity of the satanists. He convinced them that everything was under control. He admitted that those involved were wealthy and influential men, but he lied and told them that they came from another town quite far away.

He set their minds at ease by informing them that what goes on in that old, abandoned house is nothing more than a lot of harmless chanting, seances and secret passwords.

"An acceptable outlet for those who might otherwise cause harm to society," the police chief called it.

His performance was so convincing that I think the two went away almost believing that the coven was performing a valuable service to the community!

Apparently no further snooping has taken place since the first discovery. Not that it would matter anyway. Leaven has already relocated to a much more secure place, and the old abandoned house was swept clean of all evidence. We can breathe at least one sigh of relief tonight.

The Great Salvager,

Slimeball

If it feels good, do it!

To most worthless Spitwad,

Our first plan of attack against your enemy is easy and enjoyable. As you no doubt have already observed, he has been floating around on Cloud Nine ever since he made his fatal plunge into the Light. Though it pains us to no end to see him so happy, there *is* a dark lining to this silver cloud on which he floats.

Right now he is running on spiritual adrenaline. By some awful process unknown to us, new Light-lovers experience an overdose of warm fuzzies when they are released from guilt, pride and slavery to sin. The intensity of their spiritual high varies from person to person. And the more clearly they understand their new freedom, the higher their high. Age and temperament also affect their emotional state.

There are a number of benefits that this new feeling of well-being has to our ministry. Let me spell them out for you in detail lest you wallow in yet another swamp of ignorance and stupidity.

First of all, the young traitor has virtually lived his whole life up till now based on his feelings. If he feels like watching TV, he does. If he is bored and feels the need for excitement, he wanders into the kitchen and roots around for some junk food. He goes to bed when he feels like it, and, ignoring the alarm clock, rises in the morning when he feels good and ready. In other words, he is a typical teen with about as much self-discipline as a pig in a mud hole.

Now that he is an official Light-lover, he is under the delusion that life as a Christian will be a piece of cake. After all, right now he *feels* like reading the Adversary's Book. He *wants* to attend meetings at Bilgewater's church. He *enjoys* the youth group meetings and prayer times over at the Lighthouse. And since he is so gung-ho at the moment, no one has the heart to tell him that soon the honeymoon will be over.

You see, Spitwad, if he chooses to believe that his new life is just going to be one big spiritual party, then we will gladly be there to burst his balloon! For now, he knows nothing of that dangerous "walk of faith" that the advanced Light-soldiers know so well. We shall try to keep him in this state of blissful ignorance for as long as possible.

How? One way: His good feelings will soon start to fade like a smile that has to wait too long for the photographer. When that happens, we can send him down the road toward becoming a religious-experience junkie.

You can begin this process by having some of his gullible friends invite him out to their little fellowship group or to a really great Christian concert. Then someone else can encourage him to attend the new group that's just starting to meet in so-and-so's living room.

Now I realize, Spitwad, that your enemy runs the risk of actually finding some teaching that might help him. Or worse yet, there is the threat that he might meet someone who would take him under his wing and begin to disciple the teen traitor.

Next to prayer and evangelism, discipleship is certainly the most horrifying practice of the Adversary's brood.

Anyway, the danger is low because most Light-lovers think that if someone is going to Christian meetings, they must be doing okay spiritually. Besides, most of them are too preoccupied with their own lives to invest the time it takes to really spiritually care for a new believer. Aren't we glad!

Your enemy, despite his enthusiasm, is still a spiritual baby. But since he's more excited about the Light than a lot of mature believers, nobody thinks he needs much help.

Oh, he'll get a smile and a handshake, but if our other demons are doing their jobs, a commitment to be discipled by someone who really cares won't happen.

Of course, every time your enemy attends a meeting, he will feel better . . . at least for a while. In time he could become one of our prize experimental animals, pushing the religious-experience panic button every time his spiritual high begins to wear off.

There is another group of believers in the Light that we have successfully sidetracked. They live by faith in what they *feel is true* more than what *is true*. Waiting to get fixed every Sunday from their spiritual failures all week, they are stuck in the "sin, confess, sin, confess, sin, confess" spiral. In due time they will simply sin, give up and give in. Here's how it works.

One day soon your enemy will wake up feeling spiritually blah. Make sure you take advantage of that mood and implant the quiet hint, "Something is not right between me and God."

You can take that opportunity to dredge up some old, long-since-confessed sins. "Maybe I wasn't really sincere enough," you'll suggest. He will confess those sins again.

Meanwhile, the mere memory of past sins of the flesh will cause some spiritual discomfort. Then hit him—encourage his mind to journey to "Fantasy Island," where he can cruise as long as he likes on the luxury liner of his lust. Then hit him again. And again. Harder and harder.

By the time he pulls himself out of that mental tailspin he will have totally forgotten all of that "new creation in Christ" nonsense. He will be convinced more than ever that he is still a rotten, no-good, slimy sinner. And what do sinners do, my dear Spitwad? Why, sin of course!

Ah, feelings. Nothing more than feelings. . . .

It is a basic operating procedure of ours that we do everything in the darkness. As long as your Light-lover enemy keeps his struggles to himself—in the dark, hidden recesses of his heart—we have free rein to keep him in the cruelest bondage and mental torment.

To our advantage, in the evangelical church today,

more often than not, the appearance of happiness is far more acceptable than the painful progress of holiness. After all, image is everything, is it not? And honesty isn't always the best policy—especially in the church. May it remain so.

Now what would happen if your enemy, some-where along the line, actually admits to another Light-lover that he is struggling? This would happen, by the way, only if he felt he was about to explode. The other believer, unable to handle such honesty and reality, would likely deflect the cry for help with a grinning, "Well, praise the Lord anyway! I'll be sure to pray for you, David!" And so the Light-vermin will teach him the fine art of "being together, but all alone." That is the condition of many pew-sitters today.

This kind of cotton candy Christianity is all over the place, so your enemy should be able to learn quickly that "Other Christians don't have any problems—or if they do they seem to be able to work them out for themselves." This lie will prevent him from wanting to seem weird or unspiritual, so he will keep his hurts to himself.

Over time, as he learns to just "put on a happy face," he will cease to function as a "real" person. He will begin to deny his true feelings, considering them irrele-vant, as he skims along the surface of life.

Eventually, like so many others, he will fall prey to one of our inside jobs. The termites of anger, depres-sion, lust, loneliness, anxiety and fear will gnaw steadily away at the foundations of his soul, while he frantically splashes coat after coat of Christian varnish on the outside.

Spitwad, you must learn to plan with vision for the future. Yes, I know that today your enemy is full of joy in the Light. But tomorrow is a new day. Tomorrow will be *our* day.

Your silky-smooth operator,

Slimeball

Hit 'em with your best shot

To most worthless Spitwad,

Personally, in cases like your enemy, I much prefer giving our victim the shock treatment. Spitwad, you must take advantage quickly of his high feelings, low faith state of mind with a vicious blind-side shot.

Here's our chance. His parents are taking his sister across the state to spend a week with relatives there. They have foolishly placed the older traitor in charge of his younger brother and the house for the weekend.

Now, it would be nice if the two of them would simply destroy each other. Unfortunately, that probably won't happen. They are both feeling too good about themselves and each other as brothers in Christ to oblige. That alone is enough to make anyone vomit. After all, brothers are supposed to fight with each other!

All this Christian stuff and brotherly love has already given me a splitting migraine headache. Spitwad, your mere existence gives me a bad enough headache as it is! But if you can manage to pull off this simple plan of mine just this once, I might actually feel better.

Your enemy has a rather sleazy football friend who

finds his teammate's new faith to be quite amusing. Have the sleaze gather a group of like-minded rowdies and let them just happen to be in your enemy's neighborhood on Saturday night.

Make sure they have downed a few brews before making their appearance. They should be rough and ready enough by about 10 P.M.

The "brothers goody-two-shoes" will have returned home by then from their horribly wholesome trip to get ice cream . . . together. I can barely stand thinking about them.

Oh, and one more thing, Witless. Have Mr. Sleaze slip one of his favorite videos inside his jacket. You know, a little R-rated action that sizzles just enough to encourage our newest Light-lover to feel some emotions he has lately suppressed.

Don't worry. He'll be too into the plot of the movie by the time the bedroom wrestling scene occurs. He won't be able to pull away from the tube. As a matter of fact, he really won't want to pull away. His imagination will take over from there and he'll produce, direct and star in his own little video fantasy in his mind.

Later, once our guilt trap is sprung, he will realize that he was not the hero but rather the villain! Oh, our one-two punch is so sweet—make sin so exciting that he can't resist, and then kick him in the teeth for giving in!

By the way, do your best (which I know is not a lot) to make sure the younger traitor is included in all the festivities. He will feel grown-up, hanging around with the big boys. And believe me, the movie will not be wasted on him either.

You ought to be aware, my fortunate fiend, that mommy and daddy dears have issued strict orders forbidding anyone from coming into the house while they are away.

This rule will not hinder our plan. Your enemy can be easily bullied into disobeying ma and pa when the gang comes over. A few beer-belching, back-slapping "aw c'mon, man's" from our visitors and he'll give in. The pressure to be accepted and to be considered one of the guys is very strong at this age. We can use it to our advantage.

The suggestion to your enemy's mind that it would be okay to let the guys in, since he might get a chance to witness to them would really help our little deception along.

The fool can thus be tempted to disobey one command of the Light (obey your parents) in order to obey another (preach the gospel). How delicious. He should fall for that one . . . flat on his face!

By the way, make sure that the football sleazes make regular raids upon daddy dear's private, precious stash of booze.

And, oh yes, I almost forgot the final touch. After the movie is over and the two brothers are reeling from our lustful artillery fire, move in and take advantage of all the alcohol the brutes have guzzled. Prompt a couple of the bigger football goons to start discussing pro football. Two drunk high school jocks are incapable of "discussing" anything, especially when they root for different teams. A fight will quickly break out over who will win the Super Bowl, and within minutes the living room will have met its match. What is the word they use? *Thrashed.*

Do you see how simple it can be, Spitwad? This punch to your enemy's spiritual gut will knock the wind right out of him. All his warm, fuzzy feelings will be run out of town by our much healthier replacements—guilt, fear, anger, lust and confusion.

And since he has fallen into our trap of living by his feelings, we can give him a massive injection of reality. Cloud Nine will turn into a thunderhead! What blessed confusion!

The boy has bought into far more than he bargained for when he turned against us. Poor Humpty Dumpty will have a great fall. Will all the King's horses and all the King's men be able to put poor Humpty back together again? I don't think so.

And the lads won't be able to put the living room back together either!

Ah yes, the two twerps will indeed begin to feel our fury this weekend. Sunday night promises to be show time when ma and pa return from their trip. They'll be all tired out from travel and stressed out from actually having been with each other for two whole days. There will indeed be a hot time in the ol' town that night, eh Spitwad? I can hardly wait.

The two brothers will soon realize that we have just begun to fight. My old mentor, Doubt, is about ready to join you. He is expecting your enemy's house to be in perfect order for him when he arrives on Monday morning. Is that clear, Pitspit? You will see to that, won't you.

How could I ever doubt you?

Your most shocking superior,

Slimeball

A Doubt-full victory

To most worthless Spitwad,

I'm feeling great today, Spitwad, even though sending messages to you usually plunges me into depression. But nothing can spoil my mood today.

It's so good for our morale to achieve such a stunning victory. Things simply could not have gone better—even if we had written the entire script and supplied the cast ourselves!

I hope you have finally learned that *when you do what I say, things turn out right. When you try and act on your own instincts you always stink up everything!* The humorous thing is that the message I have been trying to pound into your thick skull is basically the same one the Adversary is seeking to impress upon your stubborn enemy!

Our job now is to convince the young Light-lover that his problems are merely a matter of bad luck or just not thinking or simply lack of experience.

The beauty of the whole scene Sunday night at your enemy's house was that the outbursts of anger and shock from his parents got worse and worse the more they walked around. Wasn't it just the greatest entertainment to watch Mrs. Materialist walk from lamp to vase to painting to carpet to drapes to table and so on? Each time she spotted a new disaster, her mouth would drop open a little wider and her shrieks would get a little higher!

First came mommy dear's reaction to the living room as a whole: "What in the world happened here, David?" she demanded. The two teen dweebs had made a valiant effort at covering up the scene of the crime, but it was a lost cause.

Then he tried one of our best ploys—the innocent approach, "What do you mean, mom?" That went over like the ol' lead balloon!

Then they tried to pin some of the blame on Brutus, their preppie pup. It is such fun to watch poor humans try to get themselves out of hot water by lying. They always move from *hot* water to *deep* water when they do that. And then they end up *sinking!* Great!

Mother didn't believe a word of it, of course. And she was fit to be tied when she saw the ugly stains on her new carpet and drapes. It was her worst nightmare come true. But the crowning glory of the whole scene was when daddy dear bellowed like a wounded moose upon discovering his most expensive Scotch, brandy and bourbon were gone.

The living room disaster area had been too much for him to handle and he had hurried off to find some bottled comfort . . . to fill himself with spirits, so to speak.

What wonderful revenge it all was, Spitewad! The two traitors' parents have lost all confidence in them.

When the dejected duo decided to tell the truth and spilled their guts about the drunken brawl, it got even better. Mommy and daddy were so furious that they grounded the two of them from TV, friends, phone and sports for a month.

It was music to my ears—especially when the part about the sexy video came out! I thought the two were going to be grounded from food and drink after that confession!

Like any good drama, there were a few brilliant ad libs which made the play all the more memorable. For example, when the mother discovered vomited guacamole stains on her new white lace curtains and wailed, "How could you do this to me?"—that was classic! Her tortured question was worth more than a month of our normal guilt/accusation work.

The icing on the cake came, though, at the end of the trial, judgment and sentencing. The father slowly shook his head and pronounced the most devastating condemnation: "I'm not sure I'll ever be able to trust you boys again. I had really thought you both had changed, but now I see I was wrong." Later on he slithered off to a bar, to drown his grief over the loss of his bottled buddies.

Mother's timing couldn't have been more perfect when she chimed in, "And you're supposed to be such good *Christians*." Was there not a beautiful sneer across her face when she said that hated word—Christians?

Ah yes, and so concludes another episode of our favorite family show, "Insert the Knife Deep into the

Heart and Twist." The loving family has done it again. They are so wrapped up in their precious possessions that they even amaze me with their ability to damage their so-called loved ones.

What a feast for the eyes it was to watch the two whipped puppies slink back to their rooms with their Christian tails between their legs.

Now, the younger traitor knows enough about the Light to go to his Bible to find some comfort at times like this. Yuck! Of course, he is just in walk-by-faith kindergarten, so we can still use his feelings against him.

Some of our other servants are working on him, too. Anger, Resentment and Blame will help him picture in his mind the many ways the Adversary might choose to strike down his older brother for getting him into so much trouble. He will especially enjoy some of the Psalms that describe the Light's wrath against His foes. (I don't recommend you read them before beddy-bye time, Spitwad.) Our friends will twist and turn the little lad around their fingers.

While the little Light-pest is playing the blame game, Doubt will be working on your enemy. Doubt's methods seldom vary. I expect he'll operate as usual.

Actually, Doubt feels quite at home with a Light-lover who has a steady diet of living by his feelings. When something unexpected happens to dissolve their warm fuzzies, he is able to creep in nearly unnoticed. He simply disguises himself as just another natural feeling.

His basic strategy right now is to attack your enemy's already shaky assurance of salvation. If the teen can be tricked into taking off his "helmet of salvation" (which, by the way, is already starting to fall off), we can have much freer and easier access to his mind.

He vaguely remembers hearing somewhere that our Adversary will never leave him nor forsake him. We, of course, know this to be a terrible, terrible truth from the Book. But as long as your confused enemy doubts that it is true *for him*, it will remain a truth rendered powerless to help him.

Listen as Doubt whispers into his vulnerable mind (take special note of his clever use of the first person pronoun, *I*):

How can I really be sure that Christ will never leave *me*? I'm not even sure what the Bible says about all that. Besides, I sure don't *feel* like He's there. And after the total mess I've made of things, it wouldn't surprise me a bit if He's gone. And I wouldn't blame Him either. After all, I did break one of the biggies, one of the Ten Commandments! I didn't honor my father and mother. Plus I'm guilty of corrupting the morals of a minor or something by letting Joey watch that stupid video. And, oh brother, that movie! I doubt if Christ will ever be able to look at me again after the horrible lustful thoughts I had. I sure feel raunchy. If Christ were really still in my life, I wouldn't feel this way, would I? . . .

Such delightful mind games we play. And all along, the solution to his torment lies quietly gathering dust on his desk. The Adversary will certainly try and prompt him to pick it up, but you must resist the temptation to step in, Dripwet. Doubt will counter that quickly enough. Listen to him work:

> I don't know where to even begin reading in the Bible anyway. It's such a big book filled with all that stuff about Israel and everything. And that stuff all happened thousands of years ago. How can it help me today? It would take a genius or at least a minister to really understand it. Anyway, how can I even be sure what's true in here and what isn't? It was written by men just like any other book. How am I supposed to believe that everything those guys wrote down is true?

The beauty of Doubt's work is that it is like a small snowball that starts rolling down a hill. He just gives it a little push and gravity does the rest. Soon the snowball is a snow boulder, crushing everything in its path. In the same way, our friend merely implants the smallest thought and then the human mind adds its own snow job. The seed thought of doubt gains more and more momentum, eventually sending the poor victim tumbling to the bottom of his mental and emotional avalanche.

Your teenage Light-pest will become unstable, like someone trying to walk during an earthquake or like a ship tossed around by a hurricane.

In time, unfortunately, the lad will snap out of his confusion and depression. The Adversary will see to that. Some clown enlisted by the Light will come around and encourage him. That's why we have to work quickly.

That is all part of the game of spiritual warfare. We knock him off balance. The Adversary steadies him again. And so the game continues—our side looking for the right moment to land a knock-out punch, while the Light desperately tries to train him to defend himself.

One of the strongholds that protects Doubt as he works is your enemy's relationship with his never-present father. All his life, the troubled teen has watched the back of daddy dear's head as he walked out the door . . . always going somewhere. Leaving to go to work, to play golf, to escape to the bar, to hurry off to the airport to catch a plane for a business trip . . .

Very rarely has he seen his dad coming home to him. He's usually in bed by that time or at school. Many times he has stood there in tears wishing the disappearing man would just stay for a while, hold him and talk with him. Such a sad scene; it's enough to make one dance with glee, isn't it?

Even the way Mr. Fool has disciplined him (at those rare moments) has helped our cause greatly. He becomes furious and angrily sends your enemy to his room to spend the rest of the night alone. Your brat's subconscious conclusion? If the father who he *can see* constantly leaves him and rejects him, how can he be sure the Father he *can't see* won't do the same?

For now, all the traitor knows is that when the girl evangelist read to him that gospel booklet, something good seemed to happen. The last assignment, there-fore, that Doubt will have before he oozes off into the wild blue yonder is a critical one.

He will slip the thought into your enemy's mind that maybe he really wasn't sincere enough when he prayed and asked the Risen One into his life and asked for forgiveness.

The confused boy will conclude that that is the reason why all this Christian stuff didn't stick. He will pray again to invite you-know-who into his life (though *He* never really left!). You, Spitwad, can use this act of unbelief to your advantage by being right there to provide him with some more nice, warm fuzzies.

If all goes well, you can persuade the young fool to pray that prayer every morning . . . just to make sure. Sort of like taking his daily spiritual multi-vitamin, you know. And then maybe he can be deceived into inviting Christ into his life every evening before bed . . . just in case.

Finally, we'll encourage him to do it again every time he sins . . . just to be on the safe side.

If we can bring him into this kind of bondage to his feelings and fears, we can make it so difficult for him to learn to walk by faith that he won't know which end is up. Doubting David—quite a catchy name, don't you think, Spitwad?

Undoubtedly your superior,

Slimeball

Taking the bang
out of the Book

To most worthless Spitwad,

So, the twerp reread that gospel tract the blond gave him, and now he's firmly convinced he is going to heaven when he dies. Let him. To him, eternal life simply means living forever in some faraway place called heaven after he's dead and buried. As long as he views eternal life as something he will one day receive—not as something he now has and can enjoy—we have lost very little.

Those horrible words of the Risen One: "This is eternal life: that they may know you, the only true God, and Jesus Christ whom you have sent,"[1] must never become a reality to him.

Right now, your enemy, like most Light-lovers, sees himself as basically the same person that he was before his defection to the Light. The only difference to him is that he will go to heaven when he dies. In that state of mind he presents very little threat to us.

As long as he views eternal life as just a *quantity* of life (living forever instead of just 70 or 80 years) instead of the *quality* of a life (united with the very life of God),

---

1 John 17:3 NIV

we're okay. This is one of Christianity's most basic principles, yet one of our very best kept secrets.

At this point anyway, Christianity to your teen traitor means mainly a deeper religious commitment rather than a whole new relationship with God. True, he does have a very basic understanding that the Adversary has somehow swept his sin-sick soul clean through forgiveness. But beyond that, he has little clue as to how that relationship actually grows.

Attendance at Light-infested events is his main focus right now. He thinks he has to show up at these meetings in order to find and experience God. Should he ever begin to grasp the truth that the very life and power of the Light lives *inside* him, he will become a far more dangerous pest. We must keep him from learning what the Bible really says—at all costs.

Oh, how I detest that Book! To our Adversary's people, it is like the most precious treasure waiting to be discovered. It is a sickening, fresh breeze of the cleanest, pure air blowing away our most suffocating smog of guilt and our cleverest mists of deception. It makes me choke just thinking about it.

That cursed Book is like the healthiest of health foods and most delicious of all drinks to the Light-lovers—satisfying, comforting, reviving and quenching the thirst of the most parched soul. We can't deny its power, Spitwad! Like pure lye it bleaches the dirtiest heart snow white, cures the gravest sicknesses of the spirit, and unlocks the shackles from the hearts of those we have held prisoner in the dark dungeons of sin.

If only we could burn every one of them! We've certainly tried. The Word blinds us like the most brilliant sunrise, penetrating and dispelling the deepest shadows of doubt, fear and despair. Shattering our chains into a million fragments, that horrible Laser sword of the Spirit can send us spiraling into the farthest corners of the universe . . . in an instant of time.

These are all terrifying pictures, Spongeface, but dare not *ever* forget them.

Yet there is still another ugly truth regarding our Adversary's ancient yet ever-current Book. And I must speak of it, though I can barely stomach the thought of it. Even *my* super-genius mind reels from the disgusting concept: *The Book is a personal love letter from the Light to each of his people! BARF!*

That Hated One would stoop so low as to even talk with His miserable subjects is beyond me. It is far beyond the boundaries of what is proper. He breaks all the rules! The Creator speaking with his lowly creation? It is unfair! Unfair! For His Word is . . . alive!

Most Light-lovers, fortunately, see the Book as just a bunch of letters, words, and sentences on a dry, dusty page. We're fortunate indeed.

When that Book is eaten and digested, becoming fuel for their obedient souls, it becomes like a blazing forest fire. It consumes everything in its path—all our hard work—as if it were mere dry grass.

And then (horror of horrors!), when it is energized by the Quiet One, it explodes from their hearts and mouths in deadly shrapnel of unspeakable joy, power, faith, hope and love!

I know it is too terrible to imagine, but what I am saying is all true. Oh, misery of miseries, it is all true. And it has not changed one bit over the years. The fierceness of the Word has never decreased.

With the truth of the Bible acting as a sword in His mouth, Jesus of Nazareth demolished our King's most clever temptations as though He were swatting drowsy flies. The Pure One sent our Master literally fleeing for his life. I strongly suggest you *never* remind him of that defeat!

And that same hated Book, wielded by a Light-soldier in the power and name of the Risen One, rings and sings with that same scorching song of truth. A song before which none, I repeat, *none* of us can stand. It is our kryptonite, Superstoop. And how I hate it—that living, breathing, exploding Word of God!

Now, Spitwad, you can crawl out from under the bed and stop your shivering. Pull yourself together and listen to me. Listen to these critical instructions regarding our war against the Word.

First of all, be encouraged. The Adversary's nasty Book has one major shortcoming. It is a *book*. If it were a video or interactive CD or computer game, we'd really be in trouble.

Secondly, it is not only a book, but it is a thick book. If it were a comic book with Jesus the Superhero fighting DragonBreath the evil villain of Planet X, it would be a hit. But as it is, it sits on your ex-host's desk like some unclimbable mountain peak, intimidating because of its sheer size and sacredness.

Eventually he may get his hands on one of those user-friendly paperback, teen versions. But whatever type of Bible he comes up with, it's still a book requiring active participation.

Your enemy's passive mind is programmed to respond to visual and audio stimulation that requires the least amount of energy to process. Years of parking his carcass in front of the tube have ingrained this deeply inside of him. Even when he is beating a video opponent to a pulp on the computer screen, he doesn't really have to think. He just reacts and learns by the sheer repetition of it all.

Remember, my infernally foolish fiend, a teenager's world is a cafeteria of distractions. Use that. Now that he is once again un-grounded, you can easily suggest to him all sorts of people that he really needs to call on the telephone. Even fellow Light-lovers, given enough time yacking on the phone, will run out of spiritual things to say. Then they will easily slip and slide into talking about the foolish, the trivial, and—if you work at it—the juicy world of gossip, complaining and criticizing.

Once the boy has finally made his nightly rounds of the TV, stereo, computer and telephone, it will be almost time for bed.

Soon, if you are really clever (Oh, why do I even get my hopes up!), having a "quiet time" with God and doing his homework will be doing serious battle for last place on his priority list. And since our Adversary does not hand out grades and report cards as motivation, very often the schoolwork wins out over the Word. Your enemy's parents will reinforce this way of thinking as well. This is all very beneficial and usually results in him falling asleep during quiet time—if indeed he has one at all.

Yes, it is a marvelous miracle of ours that we can turn that living, vibrant Word of God into a sleeping pill! How often has this strategy worked? I cannot even imagine. The well-meaning but exhausted Light-fool lies down on his bed, expecting to have a good time in the Word. Soon, the tired teen is sawing "Z's" with the lights still on, until mommy or daddy turns them off and tucks junior into bed.

Even in church, this spiritual reflex mechanism works like a charm. The average pew potato will be wide-awake during the singing, announcements and offering. But as soon as the minister opens his mouth to preach, it's nighty-night time for many. And who gets blamed? Not us!

Another bedtime habit of some of the more brain-dead teenage Light-lovers is to fall asleep listening to their favorite secular music. This kind of meditation we highly encourage.

It should be plain to see, Spitwit, that your job is to direct your enemy's interests and attention to anything *but* the Bible. But realize this: Our Adversary plants (unfairly, of course) impressions in the minds of His children. For some reason, He takes pity on the poor beasts and prompts them to pick up the Book and read it. In His more aggressive moments He even directs them to a specific passage to read. Brainwashing is what I call it. Pure propaganda. Anyway, that's what He does, and He does it through the one who lives inside them—the Holy Spirit.

This sort of heavenly bullying and meddling is unavoidable, so you must be ready to launch your own counterattack.

Fortunately, humans have the amazing ability to twist anything that's good. They learned this from our Most Wise Master, by the way. The Adversary's Book is no exception to this rule. There are two situations that you can turn to our advantage.

Scene One: Your enemy knows he's supposed to read the Bible because that is what Christians do. He's been told that it's good for him, but it's hard reading, and even harder to understand. He views the Word, therefore, with about as much excitement and passion as a plate of brussels sprouts.

So what do you do? Nothing at first. Let him open the Book. He will flip around looking for something interesting to read. He may close it back up again in frustration. But if he starts to read, start reminding him of all the exciting things that happened yesterday as well as the fun things he gets to do today. Frequent glances at his watch will be your clue that you are getting through to him.

Once his quiet or "devotional" time is over, he'll get up feeling like he has done his Christian duty. Within an hour or so he will be hard-pressed to even recall which book of the Bible he read from!

Scene Two: Your enemy (because of some nasty behind-the-scenes work of the Light) comes to the point where he is actually looking forward to reading that blasted Book. So what do you do? You let him read. He will probably be too into it to give in to the brute force of distraction anyway.

Deception should then be used. Very likely, he will see some verse that means something to him. That is where you move in. Quickly fill his mind with all the names and faces of other Light-lovers who "really need to know this verse."

Encourage him to congratulate himself for finding such a special nugget of truth, and for being God's instrument to help others.

But here is the key—he must not be allowed to think about the Scripture long enough to see his *own* need to apply what it says. Under normal conditions, his pride will cause him to resist any personal change anyway. That is good. We want him to learn early to hear the Word but not obey it.

It saves us a lot of time and effort when the Light-lovers deceive themselves.

If your enemy ever comes to that awful Book with a broken and teachable spirit, we'll be in deep dung.

Our King forbid that he should ever actually *do* what it says!

For now, we are safe. The treacherous brat figures he is doing enough for God by just reading the Book once in a while. He is becoming rather proud of the spiritual house he is constructing.

But our storm is brewing on the horizon. Its winds will prove to be fierce, and the pounding of its rains will be unmerciful. We will come in like a flood, and collapse his house on top of him.

Even now the barometric pressure begins to fall rapidly, and the sky grows dark. Just my kind of weather!

Your deceptive superior,

Slimeball

Seven Steps to Prayer Meeting Destruction

To most clueless and worthless Spitwad,

That irritating Lighthouse is on the move again. Curse it! It has caused my ulcer to flare up again and I have had to give up liver pâté and my favorite Château Ausone wine again.

Isn't it enough that they gather for prayer in church and in homes? Now the youth pastor has formed a before-school prayer meeting at your enemy's high school.

And it's happening all over the country! It's all because of those cursed equal access laws that allow Christian clubs to meet at the schools. Then some teen-geniuses in Texas decided to pray around their flagpole. Now there are millions of them doing it around the world! If this kind of prayer movement continues, we'll find ourselves looking down the business end of a worldwide revival!

Ooooh, I need to calm down. All this stress is killing me, Spitwad. Anyway, the fortunate thing is that not all these Christian clubs are dangerous. The ones that have lost sight of the power of prayer and have ceased to produce a bold witness on campus are of little matter to me.

The Lighthouse prayer meeting is causing trouble already. But there is more than one way to skin a prayer meeting, my foolish fiend. I understand that your enemy has been encouraged to join the blond preacher, her now-fading football flame, Steve, and a few others for morning prayer.

As you know, your teen hates the early morning and would be quite delighted if school started around 2 P.M. Now that he has to get up even earlier to pray, he will be that much grumpier. With very little prompting on your part you can help him to consider the prayer meeting as a drudgery. That's exactly what we want—for him to see it as a chore that has become an unwelcome intruder into his beloved sleep.

Soon enough, he will simply go back to ignoring his alarm clock altogether, just like before. In reality, the human lint we call "your enemy" is the least of our worries right now.

Unfortunately, the youth pastor, blond and football jock enjoy prayer and enjoy praying together. This is extremely dangerous. Let me repeat myself, Deafwit. *This is extremely dangerous!*

It is true that they have barely scratched the surface of this sickening practice of prayer, but they still connect with the Light. And He joins them in their midst when they unite their hearts. The last thing we or this school needs right now is His hot, holy breath breathing down our necks. Do I make myself clear?

I am starting to sweat just writing about it. And haven't you noticed that already there is a substantial increase in the number of angelic Light-goons hanging around campus? Do you think they are sharpening their swords for their health? Or for *ours*? Wake up!

As one of their more deadly writers once said about the Light: "He is easy to please, but hard to satisfy." Oh yes, Slipspit, He *is* pleased with this little prayer gathering, but He won't be satisfied until they turn the whole blasted high school into a Sunday school!

Right now there are seven pray-ers. Seven-and-a-half when your enemy drags himself out of bed on time. This is a large enough group to do a lot of damage to us—but it is small enough that we should be able to render it nearly powerless in short order.

The youth pastor is young, but he has been enslaved to the Light long enough to recognize some of our tricks. But not all of them! It is clear that he must be removed for our plans to succeed.

If you follow closely my *Seven Steps to Prayer Meeting Destruction*, you will do well. Pay attention.

1. Keep the purpose of the prayer meeting a vague idea in everyone's mind. Never allow them to actually focus their prayer artillery against us, nor pray about reaching the whole school for the Light.

Let them focus on feeling good about being together having fellowship and committing their day to God. They all enjoy talking to each other far more than they enjoy talking to their so-called Father anyway.

2. Make sure the meeting starts out with a lengthy sharing time. The group will heartily agree with this emphasis, perceiving their leader to be sensitive and caring. Encourage some of the more long-winded members to share at length about family medical concerns.

   A good story about Aunt Mathilda's toenail surgery or something equally ridiculous can wipe out almost an entire meeting. And no one will have the heart (or, in reality, the *guts*) to cut short the sob story.

3. Another safe topic for prayer is personal needs, especially things like upcoming exams, term papers and sporting events. Prayers like, "Lord, help me to do well on the test" or "Lord, help us to win the game today" represent a spiritual ceiling of prayer that many teenage Light-lovers have trouble moving above.

   A prayer meeting like that can easily turn into a wonderful lukewarm gathering of self-centered Light-blobs. We might even join them after a while!

4. All praise and worship is to be avoided at all costs.

And discourage members from bringing their Bibles. A few well-planted fears about being labeled nerds or fanatics will help them forget their "swords." By neglecting the Word of God, you can effectively short-circuit most prayers.

Any attempts by a member to introduce worship songs to sing as a group should be met with stunned expressions and self-conscious silence. Voices that screamed to the straining point at a basketball game the night before will fall awkwardly silent when it comes time to worship the Holy One.

Once an atmosphere of praise and worship is abandoned as uncool, the angelic goons will simply melt out of sight and out of mind. That alone would make my day.

5. Remember that prayer power is unleashed like a hurricane when Light-lovers agree together to believe and hold on to the Adversary's promises. All efforts to destroy the unity of the group are therefore extremely valuable. Here are a few tried and true techniques of accomplishing that goal:

   a. Have the outgoing, talkative ones dominate the praying, causing the more shy ones to feel resentful about not being able to get a prayer in edgewise.

   b. Cause some of the members to become irritated with one another just before the praying begins. The Quiet One will be quenched and there will be such a heaviness in the atmosphere that no one will feel like praying.

c. Gradually establish a pecking order of spirituality within the group. Those who attend most often and who are able to produce the most "Yes, Lords" from the other pray-ers will be looked upon as most spiritual. (By the way, our old friend Steve enjoys praying. He is always the first to pray and he prays long "preachy" prayers. It is hard to tell whether he is praying to the Light or to himself anymore, for he loves to hear himself talk. With a little more time and polish he should make a very, very fine Pharisee!)

6. Serious discussions about the spiritual and moral condition of others (especially fellow Light-lovers) is always welcome. Gossip hiding behind the mask of prayer requests and concerns opens the door wide for us to join the meeting—an invitation we gladly accept.

7. Finally, do your best to keep the format of the prayer meeting unchanging and unbending. Just as variety is the spice of life, so it is with prayer gatherings as well. A dry, predictable approach will kill the group out of sheer boredom—it will dwindle down to a dull duet, then die of natural causes.

   This kind of cancer generally occurs best when the leadership is non-creative and assumes a kind of protective ownership of the meeting—becoming inflexible and threatened by any suggested changes.

One more secret will benefit all your mindless meddlings in your enemy's life. Try to get him to see his faith as fulfilling a list of heavy dos and don'ts rather than a close, joyful friendship with a real person.

Help him to think, for example, in terms of "saying his prayers" instead of "talking to God." Do you see the difference, Lamebrain? It is a profound change of heart.

The first is a *ritual* approach, the second a personal *relationship*.

In conclusion, my sluggish apprentice, hear me and hear me well! The Adversary has invaded the darkness of one of our strongholds—your enemy's high school. The more the Light-lovers connect with the Source, the weaker we become. *Prayer kills*. Despite their fumbling attempts at prayer, the spiritual climate at the school is changing.

The shadows are shortening. It's getting brighter and warmer. The ice is starting to thaw. The rivers are starting to flow. Blast it, Spitwad! Do you want a flash flood on your hands?

Our Adversary has gone too far for the last time. It's no more Mr. Nice Guy for us. It's time to get down and dirty. I have just received a direct order from the bottom, though His Deceptive Majesty's plan has actually been on my mind for quite some time now.

We are sending Sleazedrip to you to do his thing,

barbaric as it is. His target? That bright-eyed, good-looking, young, and . . . restless youth pastor.

Your superior with a
superior stomach ulcer,

Slimeball

Our local
Romeo and Juliet

To most worthless Spitwad,

S ome delectable morsels are being slow-cooked in that crackpot of a prayer meeting. Ah, the aroma makes me drool! You see, the delightfully foolish youth pastor thought it would be good for developing unity in the group if they all joined hands when they prayed. How convenient for us!

Have you noticed how the girl always manages to sit next to Mr. Youth Pastor? The football jerk, Steve, has noticed, and you can see on his face how the jealousy burns inside his broken heart. He looks quite handsome dressed in the bright green of envy, wouldn't you say?

And the flirt is too infatuated with the one whose hand she holds to notice or even care what her ex-flame is going through. It's so perfect! And do you think our young, single youth pastor feels nothing when she affectionately squeezes his paw?

You can almost see her sigh with longing as she listens to him pray. She is keenly aware of how much more mature and spiritual his prayers are than those of the proud jock she once "loved."

Oh, but if this youth pastor were more perceptive, he would know what sort of woman it is that holds his hand! She is nothing but a tramp, with a history of sexual encounters that would make his ears burn.

Spitwad, don't you know who she is? Have you never figured out why the fires of lust burn so strongly inside her? Has it never occurred to you to find out about her past?

Just ask her "loving" father, my brainless bungler. Oh yes, he has indeed loved her in a way that is becoming quite the rage. Does that shock you, Splurtwimp? Well, welcome to the 90s!

This is the kind of stuff Sleazedrip slobbers over. Night after night the poor, defenseless child whimpered and hid under her covers. But always that dark shadow appeared in her doorway, hot booze-breath bearing down on her. Meanwhile, her pathetic mom cried herself to sleep in the other room, shutting her eyes and ears to it all.

Mommy's bruises, welts and broken bones were a constant testimony of what waited for the poor, victimized child if she dared raise a protest.

Her brother, boiling with rage and frustration, would put on his headphones and try to lose himself in his heavy metal music. Drowning out his sister's cries, he would pound his fist into his pillow, imagining with each driving beat that his fist was slamming into his father's face. And dreaming of how he would one day get his revenge.

We ruled that house completely until the drunken disease tired of his daughter and staggered off to find other bottles and other bodies.

Abuser, Accuser and their gang have been relentless in their mental attacks on the girl. But now that she walks with the Light in the light, she is learning about her nauseous true identity in Christ. She is able, unfortunately, to ward off most of their arrows of condemnation, guilt and hopelessness.

But she is still haunted by nightmares that one day daddy dear will come back home.

There is, however, another force within her—a deep longing that she does not understand. It is a compulsion that drives her. She yearns for a man to protect her and care for her, to hold her, love her and soothe her pain.

Oh, but the poor lamb is so confused and frightened. She is driven by this inner longing for a father's love, but Perverter clutches her heart in his vise-like grip. He squeezes and twists her yearnings for love into lust. Ah, how glorious! She is compelled to seek fulfillment in the very act that terrifies her the most! That kind of "love" from a man is the only kind she knows.

We were right on schedule with her destruction until her meddling Father in heaven began messing things up. He, in His typical syrupy, sentimental way, has made some very bold strides forward in an attempt to heal her scars.

You need to be aware that the ferocious light of His

Fatherly love has already melted down the walls of some of our most carefully constructed strongholds in her life. Perverter's grip is loosening even now. The girl is slowly learning what love *really* is. We must attack at once or we will lose any chance we have.

As for that wimpy youth pastor, he is extremely devoted to the Light. He also appears to be well-trained in the Adversary's Book. But he is a fool. He does not take us nor his own flesh seriously enough. He gives lip service to his Master's warnings about the deceitfulness of sin. He does not believe he is capable of doing anything that could be called *serious* sin. That will be his downfall.

By the way, many Light-lovers in positions of spiritual leadership are the same way. They are overly confident about their own moral purity. Oh sure, they get shaken up a bit when a well-known Light-hero falls into immorality, but they rarely take any action to protect themselves from the same fate.

Ah yes, the spirit of America lives on in the church. The rugged, pioneer spirit. The independent, capable, self-sufficient frontiersman mentality. The self-made man. The church is wonderfully gagging because its leadership knows little of *real* humble dependence on God and others. But no one seems to be around to perform the Heimlich maneuver on them. Oh pity, pity, pity.

Countless Light-soldiers have been brought down by our slow-but-steady wearing down of their defenses. The "it will never happen to me" way of thinking, especially of the younger ones, causes them to let down their guard.

Then we simply pour gasoline on their smoldering lusts through billboards, magazines, TV, movies, music and sensuous people. There is no escape from our message: "Do it all and do it now!" They struggle a bit at first, but give in to the pressure in due time.

Soon enough, our victims become like the proverbial frog in the pot—too relaxed, comfortable and drowsy to realize that the water temperature has been slowly rising to the boiling point. By the time they notice what's been going on, they don't even have the strength to hop out of the pot!

What is the key to our deception? Our good friend, Pride. You see, the higher up the Christian ladder they climb, the more important and spiritual the others believe them to be. And very often, the foolish leaders come to see themselves that way as well.

Fortunately for us, with increased responsibility often comes increased isolation. It's lonely at the top. And when the cream rises to the top, it becomes separated from the milk below. Isolated. Unprotected. Vulnerable. Prone to go sour. And when that happens, we skim the scum off the top and throw it to the dogs.

We call it the Bathsheba Syndrome. Poor King David would probably never have thought twice about Uriah's wife if his friend Jonathan had been there with him. United they stand, divided they fall down and go boom!

Our affectionate youth pastor is set up quite nicely.

He has recently burst into the youth ministry limelight through the success of that recent youth rally. His youth group is booming with new Light-lovers right now. Everyone at church is thrilled with the job he is doing. And, if the truth be known, he is quite pleased with himself as well.

Volunteers are crawling out from under the rocks everywhere to assist him and be part of the youth ministry. They jump at his every command. His boss, the senior pastor, trusts him completely, but is far too busy to spend very much time with him. So much the better for us.

Spitwad, it's time to spring the trap—brought to you by your rude and crude buddy, Sleazedrip and his supporting cast. Perverter will be working many over-time hours, trying to exploit every last bit of influence he still has in the blond bimbo.

She is an important player in this game. She is aggressive, hungry and determined. She knows in her *head* but not yet in her *heart* that God will supply all her needs. We will gladly step in and help supply all her wants. And after all, to a love-starved teen, the junk food we offer today is hard to pass up in favor of the sickening, healthy square meals the Light has promised for tomorrow.

Besides, *wants* are much more fun to fulfill than *needs* anyway, right?

Already the blond has sought out the youth pastor for counseling. She is deeply disturbed about her past, tormented by her present nightmares and fearful of the future. Plus, she also happens to have a major crush on him.

Of course, it is all very innocent right now. And nobody else even knows that the counseling is going on. The girl's mother works the night shift. Her brother is away at college. She is always the last one to leave the youth group functions and he follows her home. Perfect.

They sit in his car in her driveway until late into the night. They talk. She cries. They pray. She giggles. They hug. Oh it's all so, so innocent. But their love and affection for each other grows. And it grows in the darkness. . . .

For now, Spitwad, I want you to continue focusing your attention upon your struggling enemy. Allow Sleazedrip and the others to handle the scandal. That is their specialty. You prepare your victim for the up-coming explosion. Once the bomb goes off, there will be a lot of fallout. And if all goes as planned, the *falling out* will mean a *falling away* for him.

Do you remember what I threatened to do soon after that cursed youth rally was held? . . . when the Lighthouse began their major prayer assault on our gates? And do you recall my more recent threat that this annoying youth pastor must be removed in order for us to move forward with our plans?

I certainly hope that by now you have learned to take my words seriously, SalivaLump. I mean what I say and I say what I mean. Except when I'm lying, of course.

At long last we are on the brink of a major offensive that will kill two bothersome birds with one stone. No, I correct myself. It will kill off the whole blasted flock!

Your sleazy superior,

Slimeball

Leaven... again!

To most useless and worthless Spitwad,

That nosy nuisance of a girl knows that the police chief lied through his smiling teeth. Didn't I tell you, Spitwad, that this Leaven business would blow up right in our faces? I can smell it happening already.

How did she find out? Recently she went on one of those field trips with her U.S. Government class to City Hall. When she was walking around the grounds, she spotted one of the license plate numbers she and that jerky jock memorized the night they went Leaven-snooping. Then she spied the sign in front of the parking space: Reserved for Mayor. I thought she was going to start screaming bloody murder right there!

She's scared and doesn't know what to do. However, the little troublemaker has already spilled the beans to the youth pastor, of course. He suggested that they call the FBI, but the girl is afraid they might be in on the conspiracy as well. Amazing insight she has, isn't it?

For now, they are leaving Steve out of it. This is an awesome error on their part, and we shall take full advantage of it. But then, the happy couple is not exactly thinking clearly on a number of issues right now, eh Spitwad?

Eclipse, so says the demon grapevine, is furious. He should be. His precious operation has a serious security leak. And so he had just better take care of this matter by himself, in his own way . . . and leave us out of it!

You and I, Spitwad, wash our hands of the matter. It concerns us only because it seems destined to explode right on our heads.

As far as I'm concerned (which is not very far, I assure you!), Eclipse can go to heaven! We have important work to finish and it had better not be screwed up by Eclipse's mess.

In fact, I wouldn't be at all disappointed if there was not another eclipse of the sun for a long, long time.

Your superiorly sick superior,

Slimeball

The Quiet One

To most worthless Spitwad,

All this talk at the Lighthouse about authority, power and gifts of the Spirit is making me very uncomfortable. Things were better in the days when only the lunatic fringe of the Christian world talked of such things.

I personally prefer the churches that refer to the Quiet One as the Holy Ghost. In those places, we can sometimes convince the young Light-lovers that He is the cousin of Casper the friendly ghost or something. That's what we like—for the Holy Spirit to remain some kind of mysterious heavenly "it" or force. Just so they never discover that He is God, the third person of the Trinity, who lives within them! Oh, horrible, horrible truth!

There are some churches where the very mention of the Holy Spirit causes great worry and fear. They are so afraid of being labeled charismatic that they don't talk about the power of the Spirit at all. In so doing, they cut off the Adversary's Book from the One who inspired its writing. And since the Bible is the sword of the Spirit, they are left with the weapon but don't have the Master Swordsman to give them power to use it. Amen! May it always be so!

Unfortunately, it's not so at the Lighthouse. They are gulping down truths from the Book about the Holy Spirit like there's no tomorrow. And that includes your enemy, his stubborn brother, and now the *sister* as well!

By the way, how that miserable little girl managed to slip into the Adversary's camp right under your big nose is being thoroughly investigated by Infernal Affairs. I suspect you were too busy primping and cleaning your scales to notice that the two brothers have been praying together for their family. How could you be so stupid as to permit that? Did you think that just because they are young, the Adversary does not listen to them?

One day, as I understand it, the pesky little girl walked in on the brothers while they were praying and asked them what was going on. She felt left out and wondered why she hadn't been invited to join in on whatever they were doing. After the two explained the whole terrible ball of gospel wax to her, she simply said, "Oh, I've always hoped that were true. Now I know it is."

And that was it. Like a blasted ripe peach, she dropped right into the Adversary's palm! And not even a whimper or whisper of resistance from our side! What is going on here? Is everyone on vacation this week?

Spitwad, you can expect a visit from the Bureau of Infernal Affairs any minute. And I suggest you brace yourself. Their methods are not pleasant. Those goons make the Gestapo look like the clowns from the "Police Academy" movies. I should know. They just left my office.

Now where was I before I got distracted by that horrid little girl's defection to the Light? Oh yes, the Spirit.

It is essential that we work with all our might to keep the truths about the Quiet One hidden from your enemy's eyes and heart. You see, Spoutrump, the vast majority of Light-lovers are unaware of the awesome authority and paralyzing power they have. Generally they live like paupers when in reality they are princes.

It is to our utmost advantage for them to continue to see themselves as spiritual cripples. When they are weak in that way, we are strong.

Do you realize, my comfortable comrade, that if your enemy fully surrendered his life to the Light, he could catapult you out of your happy home and into the twilight zone in an instant? All he would have to do is speak in the Name of the Risen One and you'd be history.

Have you ever had the joy of wandering alone in the waste places? You would be whining for me to come and rescue you in no time. And do you think I actually would? Don't hold your bad breath waiting, Spitwad.

Fortunately for you, your enemy doesn't realize you are there. Plus he is still a bit confused about all this spiritual authority stuff.

Some of his fellow Light-lovers have even been lured into extremes of the Spirit and have marched right into our New Age lair. The bait? Power. You've heard them talk, I'm sure. They are constantly rebuking this, naming that, claiming this, and so on. Their motto? You possess what you confess. "Name it and claim it." Or as we say, "Gab it and grab it!"

We have tricked them into believing that they are little gods who have the power to simply speak things or visualize things into existence. It's a big ego trip for them, and a hilarious good time for us. And the fools don't even realize that they have waltzed right into the wonderfully wicked world of the occult. If we can get these idiots close to your insecure ex-host, we might have it made. Those fools can help us a lot.

When they become convinced that they are God's gift to the world, they are easily blinded to the reality that their spiritual-sounding commands are really just self-centered demands.

Since we have been able to shift the focus of their faith from being in God's Word to being in *their* word, we have cut them off from the very authority to which they so confidently appeal. How pathetic they are, yelling things at us. They are a complete bore.

Now, on the other hand, there is a very real power that the Quiet One gives to His hosts. And this is of the gravest concern to us. It has been so ever since the Day of Pentecost, when the Spirit came to dwell in believers in Christ. It makes me tremble even thinking about that awful day.

I must warn you, Spitwad. Over at the Lighthouse, hordes of them are eagerly pulling the plug on their own puny power lines and joyfully tapping into His Powerhouse, the Spirit of God Himself! In the name of our mighty Master, we must short-circuit this link!

Spitwad, something's up. All you see down here are high-level demons and bigwigs rushing around, whispering in small groups, slamming doors and meeting for hours on end with no breaks. But that's not the worst of it. This morning I was floating down the hall to the water heater to get a drink and I caught a glimpse of a shadow ducking into a board room. I had to blink my eyes to make sure I wasn't seeing things—it was Eclipse.

Your spiritual superior,

Slimeball

Divide and conquer

To most worthless Spitwad,

You have more than enough to keep you occupied at home, so concern yourself with family affairs only. See if you can't create some kind of mild panic or sense of alarm in your enemy's house. Now that Ma and Pa Materialist are outnumbered by the three traitors, a little guerrilla warfare is in order.

Why not suggest to mommy dear that they take the three children over to have a nice, friendly chat with Bilgewater—now that they are becoming more interested in religious things. Translation: Mommy is afraid the kids are going to cause her embarrassment by becoming too fanatical about all this God stuff and she just doesn't think it's healthy.

But here's the key, Spitwad. Make sure the kids go in to see the esteemed reverend one by one. By the time that puffball gets through with them, they'll each be twisted up into a doctrinal pretzel. They won't know what they believe or what *to* believe!

I have much bigger and far more important matters to attend to without worrying about the adolescent swamp gas at your house. I have been ordered to coordinate the attack on the Lighthouse.

This is the situation. Some of the more outgoing, emotional and aggressive Light-lovers are becoming spiritually bloated from an over-emphasis on the Spirit. They attend every retreat, seminar and fellowship they can get to, and greedily gulp down everything without question.

Our agents are carefully guiding them into a new blessing. Those Light-sponges will end up being neither drunk with wine nor filled with the Spirit. They will be, in a manner of speaking, drunk on the Spirit. And, as you know, intoxicated earthlings lose their inhibitions . . . and their judgment. Does this sound familiar? It should, because it has been a highly successful pattern for church division for decades.

We are making sure these kinds of conversations are popping up at the Lighthouse: "Do you speak in tongues yet, Irene? No? Oh sister, let me tell you what you are missing. Why, God has so much more for you . . ." And, "Are you filled with the Spirit, Bill? No, that's not what I mean. I'm talking about the baptism. Have you been *baptized* with the Spirit? Hmm, so I thought. Can I lay hands on you and pray? . . ."

You see, Spitwad, the goal is to divide. Divide and conquer. If we're successful, the church will soon be separated into two camps—the have's and the have-not's. Or should I say the hunters and the hunted.

In the world of over-zealous hunters, it doesn't really matter how long you have faithfully walked hand-in-hand with the Father. What matters is whether you've got "it" or not! And the "it" varies from person to person. "It" could mean an experience with the Spirit or tongues or prophecy or a certain feeling or whatever.

Certain ones in the hunted crowd will panic when they conclude that they have been missing out on something. They will quickly buy a ticket and jump on the spiritual bandwagon.

Now, as you know, there *are* legitimate gifts of the Spirit. But sometimes the Light-lovers get so excited and anxious to have it all that they manufacture it themselves.

For those who are desperate for an "experience," we will gladly supply all the supernatural feelings and gifts they could ever want. They open themselves up to us when they cease to wait for the Adversary to give them what *He* wants and begin demanding what they want.

In a matter of weeks we expect the whole Lighthouse to be in an uproar. It is all great fun, and the pastoral staff will be at a total loss as to what to do.

Splitting churches is nothing new, of course. Have you read my book on it? It's already a classic: *Splitting Heirs*. It should be required reading for every demon. In fact, I hereby require you to study it. You *can* read, can't you?

It has always been our specialty, Splitwad, to take the Adversary's tools which He designed to build up and unify, and twist them into weapons that cripple and maim.

The Light wants His puppets to cleave to Him and

to each other. We cleave them in half. Aren't we just the eager-beaver cleavers, my dull droid?

However, as they say, you ain't seen nothin' yet! While the church mice take sides and take aim at each other, their prayer cover over the congregation weakens. They will then expend far more energy debating, arguing and criticizing than they will invest in praying. So be it.

The funny thing is that the one man who has kept himself far from the flames of controversy will ultimately be the one most affected by it. I'm talking about the youth pastor. He becomes more isolated and vulnerable day by day as the prayers of the saints dwindle away.

What was it that the Light said in one of His letters to the humans? "Where you have envy and selfish ambition, there you find disorder and every evil practice."[1] Very appropriate words for this occasion, for the disorder has already begun. Every evil thing is waiting for just the right moment.

Youth Pastor Fool has appointed himself special guardian of the blond, to protect her from the angry mob at the Lighthouse. But our first missile will not hit the church. It will explode at the girl's house instead.

The orders have just come up from below. Something big is going down, and Eclipse has been given full permission to act. And what takes place will be the blast

---

1 James 3:16 NIV

that ushers in every evil thing. I can hardly wait for the fireworks to begin.

Your superior slicer and dicer,

Slimeball

The fall of the youth pastor empire

To most worthless Spitwad,

Scandal. The fragrance of that word is intoxicating. It's like perfumed poison, the sweetest scent of victory to my nostrils. Breathe deeply, my fortunate fiend, for anything but defeat has been rare these days. Let us bask in the chilling cold of this triumph and feed on the disgrace that grows on the name of the Light. For this is indeed why we exist and the very purpose for which our Master saved us!

Sleazedrip will be greatly rewarded and almost certainly promoted for his part in my sting operation. Naturally, I, being the brains behind the plan, will receive numerous awards and honors. Perhaps even our king himself will see fit to personally bestow his gifts upon me.

As for you, Stinkdip, you have merely managed to buy some more time in Suburbia, USA. That is, unless you want to request a transfer back to the jungles of Thailand? I'm sure we could arrange that right away.

By the way, how was your little get together with Attila, Genghis, and the rest of the Bureaucrats? Lovely fellows, aren't they? That Infernal Affairs gang can make anyone tremble. And I'm sure you had to change your underwear after their little chit-chat with you!

Ah, but enough of all this unpleasant talk about you. Let's go back to the far more interesting subject of me and my great victory. It was made possible, of course, by all the bitter infighting at the Lighthouse. Their prayerlessness gave us the opportunity we were looking for, and we took it. The rest is history.

Now that the sting has stung, it is safe to spell it all out for you. Prior to this we had to watch carefully lest our plans be intercepted by the angelic gangsters. One leak to the heavenly press and our whole magic bubble would have burst.

As you know, things continued to heat up at the church, with the senior pastor beside himself trying to keep order and restore unity. But a split was inevitable. The two warring factions had dug too deeply into their doctrinal trenches to give up. There was nothing the weak old man could do. His hands were full and tied. Suffice it to say, he had no time to look in after or even look in on his favorite youth pastor. Pity.

Meanwhile, things were also heating up between the lusty blond and her not-so-wonderful counselor. After all, it was only natural, with the evenings starting to turn cooler, for them to go inside her house and talk in the warm kitchen. Besides, they were starting to make real progress. The girl was remembering more of her past and opening up more to his sympathetic eyes.

Ah, but the lamp of his body, his eyes, did not stay good, did it? Soon the light within him began to fade into twilight and then to darkness. How great was that darkness!

Rationalization Central (RC) was called in and they flew an entire battalion out to the house to help ensure the couple's progress. They came up with some real beauties, too.

We had Youth Pastor Lustbucket saying to himself, "Those clowns over at church can fight all they want over theology. We're the only ones who are really loving each other, as Christ told us to." Who can argue with logic like that?

Did you happen to notice how their sessions gradually became longer and longer until finally she would drop off to sleep while they were talking? Then he would lovingly carry her up to bed, tuck her in, give her one last kiss and then leave. Ah, just like a loving daddy would do.

After a while it began to dawn on him how foolish it was to drive home at that late hour. Far better, he thought, to take a short nap on the couch and overcome some of his drowsiness than to risk falling asleep at the wheel! That sort of mental gymnastics just reeks with the smell of RC, doesn't it?

Timing was everything in this plot.

An aging professor of economics at a university across the state mysteriously suffered a severe stroke. His mid-term exam was therefore canceled.

An angry, only slightly-relieved college student tossed his bag of dirty laundry into his '82 Mustang and headed home early, to your town, Spitwad, for a long weekend. His accounting exam had been death and his history test not much better. He drove fast.

Thursday night. A mother still at work, not due home until shortly after 6 A.M.

A drowsy youth pastor blinked his eyes, glanced at his watch in the lamplight and swung his legs down off the girl's living room couch. Forty-eight minutes after two in the morning.

His thoughts began to race: "My God, I love her so much, and we're all alone in this mess." (And, my dear Spitwad, his words were not even close to being a prayer.) He slowly climbed the stairs. Warning bells were ringing all over his head, but he closed his mind to everything except his fantasies.

At the same time, an increasingly irritated, intense young driver squealed his car off the main highway and into a dark, lonely residential area. He was anxious to get home after the long drive from college. His mind was troubled by vague memories of a very evil man . . . his father.

Eclipse was on the prowl. The chill in the air, the cloud blotting out the moon. Fear clawed at the young man's stomach as he yanked the car into the driveway behind the strange vehicle parked there.

Immediately the word was broadcast over the screen of his mind in the blinding red of hatred long hidden away: "Dad!"

Racing into his mom's bedroom, he grabbed the shoebox off the top shelf of the closet. There it was, just as he knew it would be. His mom kept it there, just in case.

Suddenly he heard the hauntingly familiar muffled cries of his sister, the blond. Horrible memories of years ago flooded his thoughts and his mind exploded in rage.

At that moment in a secluded farmhouse on a heavily-guarded estate outside of town, the final prayers and malediction were being spoken by the high priest. The coven-members quivered with excitement as a hideous and unearthly roar of triumph belched from the throat of their leader.

Of course, Spitwad, the Adversary had His timing as well, didn't He? And He knew where our weak link was, didn't He, Spongebreath?

Amazing isn't it, that somehow, for some reason, He awakened your three slumbering enemies at precisely 2:58 A.M. Coincidence? Of course that's what you say! And was it also coincidence that they all started praying at the same time for the youth pastor and the girl? And they weren't even together! And was it coincidence as well that by 3:05 A.M. they were all fast asleep again, nestled all snug in their beds?

By that time, the damage had been done.

The frightened floozy's brother kicked in his sister's bedroom door, and the head of the horrified youth pastor whipped around. One gunshot and a terrified scream shattered sleepy Suburbia into a million fragments. How grand!

The bullet hit the Youth Pastor Fool in the throat, passing through the wooden headboard behind him and lodging in the wall. The cursed shot missed the girl by inches.

An invisible assassin demon swore silently and melted back into the shadows and was gone. That botch-up was the Adversary's work, no doubt. And so was the jamming of the gun after the first shot.

After that, chaos broke out. The hysterical girl, splattered with blood, flew out into the hall and into her mother's bedroom. There she downed a whole bottle of Valium, praying with all her heart that she would die.

Her brother, hypnotized by the shocking scene in front of him, stood in stunned silence as she bolted out the door.

The screaming sirens and pounding footsteps up the stairs invaded the brother's trauma of horror and he started yelling for his sister. Gun still in hand, he was grabbed by several neighbors and wrestled to the floor.

"Find my sister! I've killed him! Will somebody find my sister before she tries to kill herself?" The fool kept shouting even as the gun was torn from his grasp.

It reads like a cheap paperback novel, doesn't it, Spitwad? Or more like one of those smut, smear and sleaze grocery store tabloids. This time, however, it was real.

The shock waves have yet to fully hit that still sleeping community, but phones are already ringing in dark, secure bedrooms. And the senior pastor and his wife are even now kneeling beside their bed, weeping and praying. They were one of the first people to be called. A little late for praying, wouldn't you say, Rev?

You see, Spitwad, nobody ever expects bad things to happen to himself. Light-lovers are known for living in a Pollyanna world where everybody lives happily ever after. That's what makes them so vulnerable.

Well, we sure gave them a wake-up call they'll not soon forget, didn't we, Stinkweed? Welcome to the *real* world, Light-fools! Ha! The real world. Anger. Lust. Violence. Blood. Death. Pain. Shame. Scandal.

Murder. Where jealousy, rage and fear twist themselves together in one explosive moment in time. Suicide. When cowardice and despair sleep together. When hope is gone and help is on vacation and anger and self-pity rule.

Not exactly the kind of news the Pollyanna's expected to hear in their land of one-acre lots, tree-lined streets and fireplaces. Then again, who knows which respectable owners of those white-washed houses with fireplaces were not nestled all snug in their beds around 3 A.M. last night? The Shadow knows. . . .

If the attendance roll at a certain exclusive meeting at a certain isolated farmhouse were ever published, it would rock this town and the city like a huge earthquake! But we'll never tell, will we? . . .

And, by the way, whoever said prayers aren't answered?

Your victorious superior,

Slimeball

Where do we go from here?

To incompetent, bungling, worthless Spitwad,

They live! Thanks to your usual blundering, it appears that the lustful youth pastor *and* the lucky blond will survive. The bullet tore through the flesh of the fool's neck, but missed the vital blood vessels and spinal cord. Drat! Blood loss was considerable, but not fatal.

This all just stinks of the Adversary. The girl was saved by a stomach pump, much to her dismay. She did not want her miserable life to be spared, but the Light ordained it. We could do nothing to stop His plans.

The whole story hit the news like fire on a dry grassland. Out of control. You know how the media swarms around a good, sleazy story, especially if it involves a Light-lover. No exception here. It made the front page of both the city and suburban papers. Top story on the local TV news. It has even been the hot topic on all the local radio call-in shows. The wire services have eagerly carried it nationwide as well.

As you would expect, a certain outspoken TV talk show host downtown hasn't missed this golden opportunity to blast the whole Christian world! Good for him. Indeed, our friends in the media are to be commended for taking full advantage of the scandal.

Things couldn't be better, right? *Wrong!* I don't like it at all. Eclipse botched up the shooting. That is not like him. He miscalculated. That is not like him either. He was caught off-guard by the last-minute prayers of three weak Light-lovers.

Eclipse should have placed extra guards at your house. He counted on you, you brainless bungler, to cover that base for him. You failed. I could have told him you would. You are a miserable wretch; you always have been and you always will be. But would Eclipse listen to me? Never!

That arrogant blowhard still struts around here like he owns the place. First, his precious coven of human slaves was discovered and had to beat a hasty retreat because of the prying eyes of two snoopy teenagers. Now three twerps praying messed him up. We're being blown away by children! How embarrassing!

It is only because my hatred of Eclipse is greater than my hatred of you that you still live. I told you about my secret hideout where you now shiver—trembling for your miserable life—because I hope to deny that pompous pus-pimple the pleasure of destroying you. Someday, I hope to have that delight for myself.

I will permit you to remain there until Eclipse's wrath cools down to its usual boiling point. He is both arrogant and cruelly dangerous. *You* are an idiot and I'm tired of having to save my skin by covering up your mistakes. I despise you both. Don't think I'm being merciful, Sputumbreath. Don't deceive yourself. *You* I can use. Eclipse I want nothing to do with.

In fact, I'm counting on Leaven moving on to some other city's slime pit. They have my full permission to wallow around somewhere else.

At least we won't have to worry about the blond or youth pastor blabbing out license plate numbers for a while. The jock Light-lover, Steve, fortunately still knows nothing of the police chief's lies.

The girl is too shell-shocked to even remember the night at the abandoned house or her field trip to City Hall.

Our friendly neighborhood youth pastor is too ashamed of himself to talk. No one would listen to him anyway. I suspect that after his recovery he will quietly disappear out of Suburbia and end up in a small, rural church somewhere far, far away. If he's smart he will grow a full beard to cover up that rather nasty scar below his chin.

The blond girl refuses to press criminal charges against the Lustbreath. Oh well, we can't win 'em all. However, wherever he goes, our agents will follow him, tormenting and harassing him with guilt for the rest of his petty existence. The Light, of course, will go with him, seeking to restore him. His loyalty to His fallen soldiers is appalling to me and a supreme waste of time that I will never understand.

But that is no concern of ours. His credibility is shot, so his mouth will stay shut. That is all that matters to me right now.

So what becomes of the broken-hearted? The Lighthouse was in a shambles. I repeat . . . *was!* The whole congregation was stunned in utter shock and disbelief. But they are already regrouping. Can you believe it? The senior pastor held a meeting for the whole church during which he poured out his sorrowful soul to the weeping Light-lovers.

We could only watch through the windows. The place was like heaven, Spitwad. It was ugly. Angelic Light-goons were stationed everywhere, crying as unashamedly as the mortals. But their hands never left their swords and their tearful eyes never left ours.

The long and the short of it, is that the split in the church has been healed. Confession, repentance, forgiveness and genuine weeping were breaking out all over the place like rashes. It was too much for us well-bred demons to bear; we left after the first hour.

They went on all night. After the mourning at night came the morning of singing. Oh that horrible harmony of praise to the Light! It started with a few croaking, sobbing voices and then gathered such power that even the angels joined in! The racket was deafening. Their voices were like thunder, the flapping of their wings like a thousand hurricanes in full fury.

Even after we left that place I had to put my hands over my ears and talk constantly to try and drown them out. Our walls down here were rattling so much that I thought the whole place would cave in. It seemed to never end.

After the singing came the prayers. On and on and

on. Like hands clenched around our throats. Like brilliant flashes of light all around us—blinding us no matter which way we turned. Even the darkest corners of the abyss were lit up like a stage.

Finally it came. We all knew it would, and we dreaded it. Even our antiprayer incense gas masks could not keep out that sickening sweet scent, that deadly aroma. Choking, gagging, coughing, swearing, spitting, screaming—that's all I could hear around me and within me. The Lighthouse had connected again with the Son. And once again they had hope.

They *would* weather the storm that they had failed to see brewing on the horizon. It had crashed in on them with the most furious winds and rain. But they stand. *They stand!* They are a formidable foe, my quivering fiend.

The pastor, elders and many of the congregation have already been to the hospital to visit the youth pastor and the girl. They have asked and received of them their forgiveness for not watching out for them. They have embraced them and thrown their full support behind them for their physical, emotional and spiritual recovery. It makes me want to vomit all over them—and you!

It is all such an unbelievably nasty backlash, Spitwad, that I wonder if it was even worth the trouble.

And even though all those things are bad enough, that's not even the worst of it. Yesterday morning, the senior pastor of the Lighthouse received a phone call. It was from the pastor of the church where your enemy's granny used to go. The two men talked for the first time in years and have decided to meet regularly together . . . to pray! We can only hope they start discussing theology sometime soon.

Well, enough bad news for now. Here's the good news: Your enemy's parents have yanked the trio of traitors away from any and all involvement with the Lighthouse. I wish you could have seen the proud nod and smug smile on Bilgewater's fat face when the three lost sheep came back to his fold a few Sundays ago.

At least as precious were the self-satisfied smirks on the faces of Bilgewater's pew potatoes as they craned their stiff necks around to watch the prodigal sons and daughter walk in. It was all pure refreshment to my weary soul. Indeed I *do* experience renewal at church on occasion.

How is your enemy doing? Is he staggering from the events of the past few weeks. I'm sure he feels confused and disillusioned. He hates the youth pastor for what he did. He feels sorry for the blond and has visited her a few times in the hospital, and now at her home.

Emotionally he has clammed up. He refuses to talk to anyone about how he's really feeling about the Light, the Lighthouse or himself. He's not even really sure himself. But there is much anger locked inside of him and, I suspect, a healthy dose of fear as well.

Spitwad, I know you are anxious to get back to work. You have correctly discerned that your enemy is very vulnerable right now. But you are better off where you are. I want you out of Eclipse's sight for a while. And I want you out of my sight as well! Having your clumsy, bungling fingers touching anything at the moment is just too risky.

I have temporarily placed Droolcup as overseer of your enemy and his sad siblings. But even he has strict orders to keep his grubby hands off and let nature take its course. His role is merely to observe and report back to me any unusual behavior.

Strangely, the Light seems to be playing some kind of waiting game as well. His plans are clouded in mystery right now, but He is no doubt up to something. I fear that we may be experiencing the calm before the storm . . . *His* storm this time.

For now, the strategy we will use with your enemy is isolation. It is a technique our Most Cunning King learned from the lion (although his claim, of course, is that the lion learned it from him!).

Have you ever watched a National Geographic special? They are quite informative and much more helpful than watching those old reruns of "Bewitched" that you enjoy so much.

On the African plains, the male lion is lazy but extremely powerful. When he roars, it is so loud and terrifying that it paralyzes with fear every animal within the sound of his voice.

Meanwhile, the stalking lionesses take off after the herd of antelope or wildebeest that is the target. Instantly they single out and try to isolate one of the weak, extremely young, elderly or sick animals from the protection of the herd. The kill usually comes quickly once their prey has been cut off from the rest. The feast follows as the male lion proudly struts forward to take first share of the carcass.

Well, the lion roared in Suburbia and the media did their typically admirable job of broadcasting all the shocking smut. Your enemy's parents have helped tremendously by isolating him from the staggering herd that is fighting for its spiritual life.

The boy's confusion and anger further isolate him from the Light, as he cannot even bring himself to open the deadly Book on his desk. Though he still prays some, the heavens seem to give no response right now.

I have seen it before. It is the Adversary's way. It is His weird weaning process. He seeks to move the spiritual infants from demanding immediate answers from the Light into a more mature walk of faith. His goal is to teach them a lifestyle of waiting, resting, trusting and walking with Him.

We simply can't let Him succeed in your enemy's case.

The Quiet One has led the brat into the wilderness. I'm sure the kid is feeling confused, disillusioned and isolated. And so, to our way of thinking, the weak one has been cut off from the protection of the herd.

Our lionesses are crouching in the shadows waiting . . . waiting in the hidden places in the wilderness until just the right moment. Every one of our muscles and sinews are wound tight like a coil, ready to pounce.

The lion will roar again, and then the chase will be on. The feast will quickly follow, Spitwad. We may even let you come out from under your rock and eat. But not until I have first had my fill.

Your lion-hearted superior,

Slimeball

Peer pressure, persecution-style

To most worthless, exiled Spitwad,

It is music to my ears and a delight to my eyes, Spinewit. The hallways and classrooms of Suburbia High School are humming with the hatred of a teen world that feels it has been given a new lease on life. Or should I say a new lease on *lust?*

How many times, I wonder, has the word "hypocrite" been uttered in the past month or so? How many times has a known Light-lover slinked over to his locker only to hear snickering behind his back as heads quickly turned away? How many eyeballs have rolled in disgust whenever anything to do with the Lighthouse was mentioned?

The answer, my fiend, is blowing in the wind . . . It's a continual nightmare for anyone who was ever publicly associated with that church, the youth pastor or the Light Himself.

Isn't it amazing how quickly something *horrible* to the human pests can become a source of *humor,* especially when it involves the Adversary? I like it. No, I love it!

You see, ever since the youth rally, the cowardly

teens at school had felt the hot breath of the Quiet One's pursuit. Students had been dropping like flies into the Enemy's camp and the student prayer meeting had been growing steadily.

But since the scandal, the teens have found a new justification for their self-centered lives. After all, they say, the youth pastor turned out to be a fraud, right? Therefore, they reason, all this stuff about God and Jesus must be a farce, too. That's *my* kind of logic.

So what have the teenage animals at school done? They have thrown an unofficial party of freedom, pouring out the most merciless humiliation on any and every Light-lover they can. Now I wonder, where in the world did they ever come up with the idea of *persecution?*

Stumbling into this hostile world every day is your sleepy-eyed enemy. What is he hearing over and over again? What message attacks his mind all day long? "You were a real jerk to listen to those people, David!" "You were taken in, just like the rest of them." "Hey, you don't still buy all that God stuff, do you?" "Why don't you just leave that mess behind you. Forget about it now. You used to be a real cool kid." "Sure, you made a mistake being involved with those people. That's obvious. But we all blow it sometimes. Listen, we're having a party Saturday night. Why don't you come on over?" "Hey, Dave, welcome back to the real world. We were really worried about you. C'mon and party with us!" And so on.

And what conclusion do you think he's drawing in

the face of this relentless barrage of pressure? He's saying to himself, "Maybe they're right. Maybe Reverend Bilgewater is right. Maybe all along they were right and I've been wrong."

You see, Spitwad, our goal is not to make an atheist out of the boy and try to convince him that the Risen One never existed. That's simply not necessary and maybe not possible.

We don't even need to try and persuade him that his conversion was just an emotional high. He's come too far for that anyway. He would never fall for it. In fact, he might snap out of his stupor, wake up from our hypnotic spell, and laugh in our face as he raced back to the Light.

No, our plan is far more devious than that. Our strategy right now is not to *destroy* his faith, but to *dilute* it. Later on, if he wants to crash on skidrow, he can be our guest. For the present, however, we want him to simply melt into the scenery—to become a Christian chameleon who can change colors to match those around him. To just stay quiet about his faith for a while. To create no waves. Just go with the flow . . . for self-preservation, of course.

For example, when his sleazy football friends tell the latest youth pastor joke, we want your enemy to be able to laugh with them. Self-preservation. It will help him to rationalize, "Hey, those guys aren't so bad. Sure they're a little crude, but at least they're not hypocrites. Besides, they are starting to accept me again, and that feels really good."

When he sees the other Christian kids on campus who are staggering under the same persecution that he is, he can smile at them, tell them he's doing okay and quickly move on. Self-preservation again. He'll think, "Man, I just can't be too buddy-buddy with the other believers right now. It's not worth the hassle. Plus, I'm just starting to be able to hold my head up high again in these stupid halls."

Do you get the idea? We are succeeding in convincing him that it's just too draining to buck the current and swim upstream. It's soooo much easier to just let go and float.

Ah, it is so much more relaxing to just let the warm tide wash over your weary soul and carry you away. To where? Who cares? As long as friends are there, what does it matter? It's so peaceful and so, so good to see the smiles on the faces of others at school once again . . .

And Spitwad, the one thing your enemy does not see is that their smiles are not smiles of the living but are grimaces of the dead. And behind those laughing eyes lie the blank stares of lifelessness. The current that carries his friends along is gradually going to speed up and carry them over the waterfall. And he'll go with them. How marvelous!

No, Sludgepit, it is not necessary to turn Light-lovers into worshipers of our Most Worthy Master in order to defeat them. We just need to keep chasing them until they get too tired to run anymore. And when they stop fighting, we start feeding.

Compromise is always the most effective road to conquest. Give in. Give up. Sell out. Once the cowards are over the first hump, it is all downhill from there. And guess who waits at the bottom, licking their chops?

Now is the time to move and move we have. Remember, the best jokes grow old quickly and the juiciest news becomes cold and dry in no time. And high school life moves on. Soon the Lighthouse and youth pastor episode will be ancient history and the persecution will die out.

That's why the helpful habits of compromise need to be forming in your enemy right now. So when the floodwaters recede and life returns to normal, he will be so used to floating down the stream of life hidden in the Christian closet, that he will never want to leave that comfortable darkness again.

Sure he'll end up in heaven when he dies. There's not a thing we can do about that now. But he won't take anybody with him. And that is victory enough.

Your "kicking back" superior,

Slimeball

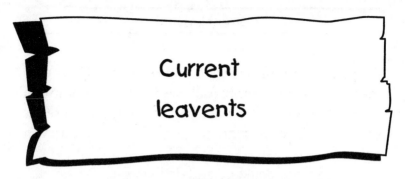

Current leavents

To most worthless and worrisome Spitwad,

S pitwad, I am tired of your constant pestering about what is going on with Leaven. I have told you repeatedly that I would relay to you any information that I received. Not that I have the least bit of childish curiosity about ritual sacrifices and dark, midnight masses that you obviously do. I haven't really been thinking about Eclipse and company at all.

The football jerk, Steve, came to visit the blond at her home. He, unfortunately, seems to have been genuinely humbled through this whole business, and seems to be stubbornly clinging to his faith. In fact, it appears that he is getting stronger. He is not swayed nearly so much by public opinion as is your enemy.

The jock now knows our little secret—that Leaven has been very active on a local level—including the city mayor's office. That's the latest I have heard. Personally, I try not to concern myself with the possible problems that girl and the others could cause.

Emotionally, she is still a basketcase. The youth pastor has dropped out of sight as expected. And the football fool is no hero, at least not by himself. So Leaven's little secret seems to be safe and secure.

And so, by the way, are you. At least for the moment. You are to report back for full-time duty in the morning. Eclipse is off tending to his flocks in other states. I suspect that he has forgotten that you even exist.

I wish that I could go and do likewise.

Your reluctant superior,

Slimeball

To most worthless and unwelcome Spitwad,

Have you ever noticed, Spitwad, how birds never fly before a summer storm? They just sit on the power lines, waiting. The Adversary's angelic-goons are acting like that and they are driving me crazy! No activity. No plan. Nothing. They're all just standing around sharpening their swords. Hour after infuriating hour.

Knowing your incredible stupidity, you probably feel this is a good time to catch up on some of the old episodes of "I Dream of Jeannie" that you missed while in hiding. Need I remind you that our Ever-Watchful King never ceases creating and carrying out his brilliant schemes?

The Light-warriors may choose idleness, but we are not so lazy as they!

By the way, speaking of idleness, what were *you* doing when that nuisance, Steve, came over unannounced to your house to visit your enemy, David? Why did you not alert me? Did you think he was coming over for tea and biscuits?

I expected your mealy-mouthed excuse—"It was as if some invisible restraining hand kept me quiet. I couldn't interfere, I couldn't move and I couldn't call for help." What you are describing is that brazen practice of *binding* us in the Name of the Risen One.

But did that really happen to you? I doubt it. Every demon-worm like yourself pulls that excuse out when he's really in a bind. Don't think I was cast out of heaven yesterday, Suckwart!

More than likely you were so absorbed in the latest Stephen King novel that you never even noticed what was happening right under your ugly beak!

Once again, if not for my brilliant foresight in planting the RDU (Remote Detection Unit) in your enemy's house while you were away, their entire conversation might have been lost to us. As it is, I shall replay the key parts of the whole painful episode for you so that you can know the shaky ground on which you now fidget. I suggest you renew your passport.

This is the transcript of the conversation recorded from the time your rather shocked enemy opened the door and stupidly allowed a very concerned football twerp into your house.

Enemy: Steve! Hi, uh . . . I mean, I didn't expect you or anything.

Jock: I know, and I'm sorry about dropping in like this, Dave. But it was one of those spur of the moment things. Uh . . . can I come in for a few minutes?

Enemy: Oh sure. Sorry. It's cold out there. Come on in.

Jock: Thanks. Hmm . . . is there someplace you and I can talk by ourselves?

Enemy: Yeah, sure. Come on up to my room. It's kind of a mess, but Joey and Sherry won't bother us there. Not if they know what's good for them!

Jock: Dave, listen. I don't want to beat around the bush, okay? I'm here because I'm really worried about a few things.

Enemy: Like what?

Jock: Like us.

Enemy: Us?

Jock: The group, you know. All the Christians at school . . . especially you.

Enemy: Me? Listen, Steve, you don't have to worry about me. I still pray and stuff and I'm going to church. Joey and Sherry and me, we talk sometimes, too.

Jock: Dave, knock it off. You're back-pedaling on oil. You don't believe that bunch of garbage you just fed me anymore than I do. Listen, we're all scared of what's happening. Our little bubble burst right in our faces, and that's too bad. But we can't do anything about that now. We can't just crawl into our holes and hide.

Enemy: Who's crawling?

Jock: Come off it, Dave. I'm not blind. I see what you're doing. You're going to all the "right" parties again, hanging around the studs on the team, laughing at their jokes . . . pretending you

227

were never a Christian at all. Don't you think God sees what you're trying to do? I mean, I see it. Don't you think *He* does too?

Enemy: Hey, who are you to judge me, Mr. High-and-Mighty?

Jock: Dave, c'mon buddy. We're on the same side, remember? I'm not saying I haven't had my problems recently, because believe me, I have. God has been hitting me right between the eyes with how prideful I've been. But you and I . . . we're supposed to be brothers, but we've been acting like strangers. I'm just concerned about you, that's all.

Enemy: Well, what am I supposed to do? You've heard all the jokes, the cuts, the snide remarks. You got it as much as I did, maybe more since you and Jennifer were . . . used to be seeing each other. As Christians, I mean. Didn't all that garbage bother you?

Jock: Yeah.

Enemy: So why didn't you . . . um . . . crack under the pressure like I did?

Jock: I'm not sure. Maybe it's because I held on to something that I think maybe you forgot.

Enemy: What's that?

Jock: Romans 8:28

Enemy: Huh?

Jock: "And we know that in all things God works for the good of those who love him, who have been called according to his purpose."

Enemy: So what's that got to do with anything?

Jock: Well, the way I see it, if God can still bring good into my life . . . our lives . . . through this whole mess—the split at church, the shooting, Jennifer taking all those pills, even the persecution at school—then that means God is still on His throne.

Enemy: And?

Jock: And if I keep trusting in Him, even though times are really tough right now, then I'm going to come out ahead in the end. Because God promises to turn this all for good. He is in control, the devil isn't. And God never loses in the end.

Enemy: Well, it sure seems like we've lost.

Jock: A battle maybe, but not the war. Jesus has already won the war.

Enemy: What war?

Jock: The war we're in right now. The war between God and Satan, good and evil. C'mon Dave, you can't have forgotten all the teaching at church on our identity in Christ and spiritual warfare already? Satan is a defeated foe and Christ defeated him and we are *in Christ!* We have died to sin and have been raised to walk in newness of life with Him. And we are seated with Christ in His position of authority over the devil! We are more than conquerors through Him who loves us! I know you missed the end of the conference when they walked us through the

"Steps to Freedom in Christ," but some of that stuff had to stick with you.

Enemy: Obviously not as much as stuck with you, preacher man.

Jock: Dave, I'm not here to preach to you. I'm here to ask for your help.

Enemy: You can't be serious. . . . You *are* serious. How can I help *you*? I'm the one who needs the help!

Spitwad, I can't stomach listening to any more of this right now. I've already had to endure it once already. That cursed conversation goes on for another couple of hours as your enemy practically crawls on his miserable belly back to the Light. It's enough to make *me* want to go to Thailand.

A lot of the prayer that comes up next on the recording is, fortunately, too difficult to hear. A whole swarm of angels decided to show up and join the two. A few of the angelic hams must have discovered the RDU because they started singing praises to the Adversary right into the microphone. At the top of their voices. Real cute.

As best I can determine, the jerk went through a good part of those troublesome *"Steps to Freedom in Christ"* with your enemy. He encouraged him to finish them by himself later on. If he does, Slipshod, *you're* finished.

Suffice it to say, the worst damage has been done. Your ex-host is back on track with the Light. So what will you do, you wretched rat, now that the garbage in the boy's life is being removed? Maybe you can jump into their trash compactor!

Your Light-lover teen is on the brink of becoming truly filled with the Quiet One's power. Will you seek to match wits with *Him* again? You lost miserably before; you will lose again.

Your enemy is almost ready for battle. Perhaps you *would* be better off going back to dear Mr. King's latest novel. Maybe you'll learn something.

Oh, one more thing. The last bit of the RDU recording is crystal clear. You need to hear it, Fizzleface.

Enemy: A while ago you said something about asking for my help. Maybe I'm a little more ready than before to hear about that. What's going on?

Jock: Are you sure you want to know?

Enemy: No, but go ahead anyway.

Jock: Okay. Last year Jennifer and I were coming home late from a date and we spotted a car going into the woods off Claytonville-Briggs Road. About two miles north of where Route 158 comes in.

Enemy: So?

Jock: So we followed the car and found it parked with about ten or more other cars at an old abandoned house back in the woods. There was some kind of satanic meeting going on in that house.

Enemy: No way!

231

Jock: Yes way.

Enemy: So what'd you do?

Jock: What do you think we did? We got out of there as fast as we could. But not before we managed to memorize three license plate numbers off the cars that were there. That place was crawling with money, Dave—Beamers, Mercedeses, Jags.

Enemy: Whew. So then what happened?

Jock: Jennifer and I reported what we saw to the police chief, but he assured us it was all under control, and that nobody from around here was involved or anything. He said that nothing really harmful was going on out there, and that they were keeping an eye on it. He told us not to worry.

Enemy: Well, that's a rel—wait a minute. He was lying?

Jock: Through his capped teeth.

Enemy: How do you know that for sure?

Jock: Jennifer, before the shooting that is, went downtown to City Hall on a field trip and saw Mayor Townsend's car.

Enemy: Big deal. So what?

Jock: The license plate number on his car matched one of the three we memorized out at the old house.

Enemy: My God!

Jock: Something's got to be done, Dave. That's what the police chief wanted us to believe. I really think we may have hit on something big—like

the answer to those weird kidnappings of prostitutes in the city. And remember the Halloween
abduction of that kid a few years ago?

Enemy: Yeah, I never believed that story about it
being his stepfather grabbing him. It was too
weird.

Jock: So, how about it? Will you help me do something? I have no idea yet what I'll do, but I can't
do it alone. I know that much. For starters, I need
someone I can trust to keep this a secret and
who will pray with me. So, are you in or out?

Enemy: I'm in, bud.

For your information, Spitwad, the jock's dad is in,
too, and he has talked to the FBI in the city and explained the whole thing. Some of the members of the
Lighthouse work for the feds. But not to worry. The
Futile Bureau of Incompetence is the least of our worries. Leaven is there.

Eclipse had to be alerted to these new develop-
ments. I had no choice. A plan of his is already in
motion. The license plate number on the jock's car has
been traced by our friend, the thirteenth Leavenite.

I distinctly hear thunder rolling in the distance. The
birds on the wire seem to be getting a little restless. The
air is deadly calm. I don't think I like it.

Your nail-biting superior,

Slimeball

233

You did what?

To most imbecilic Spitwad,

No, operator, I will *not* accept the charges! Spitwad, is that you? Oh, stop your whining, Skunkbreath. Operator, charge this call to the account of one Spitwad Q. Imbecile!

Yes, Spitwad, I'm still here. Where are you? What happened? What do you mean, your enemy told you to leave? What you're really saying is that he told you to leave him forever and to go where the Lord Jesus sends you, right? Ah ha! *That* explains why there is so much static on the line.

So, my homeless fiend, how do you like the waste places by now? . . . Yes, yes, I know you must be very lonely. Believe me, my heart is just gushing over with sympathy for you. Okay, okay, now just slow down and tell me the whole story.

I see . . . soon after his meeting with Steve the dweeb, you began to whisper not-so-sweet nothings into your enemy's ear? . . . Uh huh . . . yes, well, you *say* that you were careful and did not come on too strong too fast. But I wonder. So what exactly did you say to him?

"Nothing has really changed. I'm still the same,

wimpy Christian I always was"? Pretty good start, Spitwad. I'm mildly impressed. *Then* what did you say to him?

Okay, you said, "Who do I think I'm fooling? Three hours of talking with somebody can't possibly make that much of a difference. After all, it takes a lifetime to become a really strong Christian."

Very good, Spitwad. That was an excellent use of half-truth and the use of "I." You may have actually learned a thing or two from me after all.

So what was his reaction? Doubt was beginning to take hold again, I can see. So go on, what did you say to him next? Ah, the ol' doubt/guilt one-two punch. Good. Good. What? The connection is crackling a bit. Wait a minute. Okay, repeat what you just mumbled.

"God maybe has forgiven my sins, but He knows He can't trust me yet. Especially with anything really important. I'd better not jump too quickly back into this whole thing or I might just fall again." That's not bad, Spitwad, but I would have said something like: "Sure God has forgiven me, but everybody at school knows what a hypocrite I am. If I suddenly appear at school like I'm Mr. Super Christian . . . like Steve . . . then they'll all just be on my case even worse than before!"

Anyway, what's done is done. So far you have yet to give me any explanation as to why he suddenly turned on you. Okay, okay. So next you tried to amplify his sense of weakness and inadequacy through fear and intimidation. What *exactly* did you say to him?

"And what in the world was I doing when I agreed

to help Steve with his personal war against the satanists? I must be crazy! Those people have knives and stuff. What have I gotten myself into? I could be killed!" Sounds good. By this time, Spitwad, he should have been well on his way toward becoming a total spiritual and emotional basketcase. He had obviously forgotten all that nonsense about his being a child of God. So what happened? How did you manage to blow it this time?

Knowing you, Splitweed, you were probably feeling pretty pleased with yourself at that point, weren't you? Uh huh. And so, you decided to do something really bold and risky, right? . . . Oh shut up! I know you all too well. I can smell it coming. What? Oh all right, all right.

I see . . . in true demon style you figured you ought to kick him while he was down. I'm listening. You whispered in his ear and . . .

"I really am a failure at this Christian thing. I've never really been good at much of anything, come to think of it. I'm a second-stringer all the way. My grades are second string. I play second string football. I came in second for senior class president. I'm just following the same old Dave lifestyle by being a second string Christian. Bench warmer. Born loser. I don't

236

pray even close to as much as I should. I'm afraid to share my faith. Am I *really* filled with the Spirit? I don't feel any different. I don't read my Bible very much . . ."

Hold it right there, Spamzit! You were doing just wonderfully in the accusation department until you brought up the Bible. What did your enemy do when you reminded him that he hadn't been reading that cursed Light Book? That's right, you ninny. Of course he looked over at it. What did you expect him to do? How can you be so brainless?

You walked right into the Adversary's trap. You had your enemy beautifully focused inward, wallowing in the muck and mire of self pity. And then you blew it.

Did you learn nothing from the master strategy of Our Most Cunning Lord? Did he not direct the foolish first woman's eyes to the one thing which she was *not* to have? But not you . . . oh no. You had to direct your enemy's attention to the one thing which he needed!

You are an absolute idiot! You had him staggering on the ropes, unable to defend himself against the knockout punch, and then you pointed him directly to the way of escape!

Did he then, by any chance, get out of his chair, walk over and pick it up? He *did?* Gee, I wonder why he would have done such a thing? . . . What did you say? You don't know? Because you practically told him to, you fool!

And so he read from the Book. Oh, and *then* he mysteriously decided to finish going through those awful *Steps to Freedom in Christ*, did he? And then you, no doubt, began to panic, didn't you? Didn't you? . . . Who me? Angry? No, no, far be it from me to even *think* about getting angry with you. I'm not angry. *I'm furious!*

Yes, I do want you to continue your tale of woe. I'm all ears, Spitwad. But do speak up a bit, the phone lines out to where you are have been chewed on by so many frightened demons that the static is almost impenetrable.

So, you made the snap decision that your enemy needed to be distracted from his pursuit of freedom in Christ? Brilliant deduction, Sherlock.

And how did you propose to shut the barn door after the horse was already out? Huh? What did you say? You want me to repeat the line about the horse? Forget it, just forget it. Go on.

Ah, so you figured that you would try some scare tactics and reveal your presence to him. You've been wanting to do that for so long, I know. Just a quick materialization, I see. Nothing too dramatic. Just a chilling sense of something evil. Uh huh. Just enough to strike some terror in his heart and maybe cause a panic attack, right?

Well, what I want to know is, why didn't you *fully* unveil yourself to the boy? He would have started laughing so hard you could have escaped!

Oh poor, poor Spoutwoe. I see that your sad, sad story is drawing to its predictable conclusion. Instead of being frightened silly, your enemy exercised his authority over you in Christ. And so you find yourself there in an isolated phone booth in the middle of spiritual nowhere-land.

No, I will not come and get you. No, I will not tell you how to get back. You will eventually find that way yourself. Those are the rules, and I can do nothing to change them.

I suppose I should tell you, though, where our Adversary happened to direct the teen to read in that horrible Book of His. I checked. It was James 4:7: "Submit yourselves, then, to God. Resist the devil, and he will flee from you."[1] It's so hard to quote this stuff. You ought to read it sometime . . . and weep.

Before I do what I should have done long ago—hang up on you—I suppose it wouldn't hurt to give you a little good news.

You will be quite interested to hear about the progress our dear friend Eclipse and his pack of Leaven-wolves have made. They are taking some strong steps to preserve their little secret.

A certain Suburbia High School football coach was paid a considerable sum of money to do a little behind-the-scenes service for the cause.

The other day he slipped away from football practice for about ten minutes, supposedly to make an important phone call . . . something about some new equipment for the team that had been delayed in arriving. That was his story anyway. Nothing unusual. The assistant coaches were actually quite glad to have that tyrant off their backs for a few minutes anyway.

Unseen by any human eyes, our coach-puppet stole

---

1 NIV

around to the back parking lot where a certain Light-lover jock's car was parked. What, Spitwad? No, I'm talking about Steve here, not your enemy.

Where was I? Oh, yes. What a pity the poor lad had no car alarm system. The coach was able to get into the car quite easily. Then a half dozen or so joints of a particular sweet-smelling but illegal weed were carefully placed in the glove compartment of that vehicle. And a half-smoked one was placed partially visible in a backseat ashtray. And then the shadowy figure simply slithered back to the field, no one the wiser.

Strange coincidence, you know. There was an anonymous phone tip to the police chief. A squad car was sent out. A shocked and embarrassed football player was pulled over on his way home from practice. The officer, peering in through the window, just happened to spot the joint in the ashtray.

The Light-pest was brought in for questioning and almost had everyone convinced of his innocence. That is, until a thorough search of the car was conducted.

Yes, my dear, lonely Spitwad, I'd say that boy Steve is in a heap of trouble. And so, I really don't think he is going to give the poor Leaven folk any more grief for a while.

After all, who's going to believe some crazy midnight story from a pot-smoking jock or a suicidal teenage girl or a sex-crazed youth pastor?

That makes three down and two to go—your enemy and the jock's dad. I believe Eclipse wants very much to take care of number four personally.

The last time he tried something like this, he failed. He will not fail again.

Our triumph is near!

The ringing of a telephone in an isolated phone booth somewhere in the middle of nowhere shatters the dusty stillness

Hello, may I speak with—¿ What do you mean, "Joe's Pizza"¿ There's no pizza pla . . . oh, very funny, Pastabreath. Listen, you dimwit, this is no time for fun and games. Things are breaking fast and furious at your enemy's house.

We, of course, have all our audio and infrared video units set up all over the place. I have eight monitors set up in front of me so that I can watch the action live and relay to you what is happening the moment it happens.

Huh¿ Why are we . . . ¿ Oh, that's right. You're clueless as usual as to what has been going on. Well, okay, we've got a few minutes here before the fireworks begin. I'll try to bring you up to speed.

It's now about 1:15 in the morning in snoozing Suburbia. What¿ Your Mickey Mouse watch stopped¿ I don't care. Listen, Spitwad, there just isn't time for your usual mindless interruptions, so just chew on your tongue and listen for a change.

Leaven is throwing another one of their parties right

now, complete with all the holiday trimmings. It promises to be a bloody good show, I assure you.

Right now, as I look at the monitors, things seem to be pretty quiet around your old homestead. A few bored-looking angels are standing guard as usual. I *do* wish they'd stop grinning into our cameras. It's very annoying.

I'm a bit surprised, actually, that our Adversary has not posted more guards than this. You see, Spitwad, your enemy's mommy and daddy are gone for the weekend. That surprises you, eh? Well, daddy dear's boss felt he needed a weekend away from everything. The poor old boy has been a bit stressed lately (which, in his case, means he's been hitting the bottle too much!).

Does a weekend at the Hyatt downtown sound nice? And all arranged and paid for by your friendly neighborhood Leaven-puppets.

They were only willing to go away if someone they knew and trusted stayed with the trio. So guess who's spending the weekend? The jock and his little jockling brother! We couldn't be happier. It makes everything so much cleaner.

Your enemy's parents could not have cared less that Steve was out on bail for possession of marijuana. They've been smoking the stinking weed themselves ever since Woodstock! I tell you, Dopehead, the whole blasted town is going to pot! Either that or they're going to crack! I guess you could call them all a bunch of crackpots, eh, Spitwad? Get it? No, of course you don't.

Huh? Why all the camera equipment? Well, actually it's now standard operating procedure at any Light-lover home or hangout. It frees up some of our agents to go elsewhere instead of having to do constant stake-out duty.

See what great improvements you miss when you spend a few weeks sucking your thumb in the twilight zone?

We've also got cameras sending back pictures from the Lighthouse. Of course, that place is dark and deserted at this hour, but tomorrow morni—

Wait a minute. Hold the phone. There are headlights. One, two, three . . . ten . . . over twenty cars just pulled into that church's parking lot.

Dozens of Light-soldiers are hurrying into the Lighthouse! At this hour? Why? What is going . . . *NO!* It's a prayer meeting! Has there been a leak in our security? How could they . . . ?

The transmissions from the Lighthouse just went dead. That miserable technical crew they sent over there. They couldn't defend a fire hydrant from a blind basset hound to save their scrawny necks! Angelic Light-goons slashed them into oblivion, no doubt—reinforcements must be sent immediately. That meeting must be disrupted! Just wait a minute, Spitwad. Yes, yes, yes! I'm getting to that. I'm checking the monitors at your enemy's house to see what's going on over there. The Light-guards seem to be getting some new orders or something. They're huddling together, all of them yammering excitedly at the same time. Their leader seems nervous. What? They're gone. Poof! They just all took off, a fading comet of light streaking west.

Ah, they're headed for the Lighthouse. Our Adversary correctly anticipates our counterattack there. Well, let them go. They are all fools.

Hello? Hello? No, this is *not* a party line, lady. And if you know what's good for you, you'll get off the phone, mind your own business and go back to bed. How would you like us to haunt your cheap, stucco house? What? Well, the same to you!

Can you believe that, Spitwad? She had the nerve to hang up on *me?* What? Yes, I know I wasn't very nice to her. Demons aren't *supposed* to be nice—

Ooooh baby, here we go. The feature film is about to begin. I'm watching it all on my monitors. Just now, outside your enemy's house a street light just popped. Next come the phone lines. . . . Excellent, excellent. Now the power gets shut down.

This guy is *good.* I understand he was flown in from overseas. High-level stuff! You should see it now. The whole area around your enemy's house is as dark as death. And Eclipse is hovering over the whole block like a giant, black vulture.

And, oh, how sweet. The dear little children—all five of them—are nestled all snug in their beds, while outside lurks an enemy the bravest men dread.

The plan, my banished bonehead, is for it to look like some psycho, acting alone and only for himself, did the hit. Swiftly, silently, cleanly, they will all die at his hand. The fifth will be saved for an eager group of Leaven.

The assassin will finish the job, then drive to a prearranged spot out in the country. A messenger from Leaven will arrive soon after, leaving a briefcase of cash in untraceable bills at a place near by. The messenger will then report immediately to Leaven confirming that all had gone according to plan.

It will all be over in less than an hour-and-a-half. The Leavenites will all be far away long before the jock's parents come to pick up the poor slaughtered lambs for church in the morning.

And the assassin? He will be winging his way south on an early flight to a remote Caribbean Island owned and operated by a very loyal and very wealthy Leaven-puppet—but not before he makes his mark on your enemy's house.

His name will soon be a household word, striking terror into the hearts of a thousand Suburbias coast to coast. This will indeed be our finest hour.

Our friend, Omega, is already cutting through one of the window panes in the downstair's den. He has barely made a sound so far. Not even Brutus, who sleeps out back, has been spooked.

He will soon be inside, penlight in his left hand, his silenced semi-automatic handgun in his right.

He's standing up in the den now, Spitwad, looking around and assuring himself that all is indeed quiet on the western front.

It is.

He has the quickness and strength of a panther. He even *looks* like an assassin is supposed to look. Dull black turtleneck, black slacks, black ski mask, black gloves, black shoes. He could be Eclipse in human form.

He's moving rapidly now through the living room, his eyes glancing everywhere, but his destination very clear. He's headed for the stairway.

Climbing slowly, carefully, trying to avoid any squeaks that could startle the sleeping saints, his first stop should be your enemy's room.

Wait! Omega must have heard a noise downstairs. I heard it, too. A door opening? I don't know. Aaaaauuugh! My eyes, Spitwad! All eight monitors have turned blinding white!

Where is Eclipse? What is happening? Hold it, I can faintly see on one monitor. Omega is crouching, popping a fresh, new clip into his gun. He's starting to move cautiously toward the stairs.

No! Angels! Light-warriors everywhere! Their faces are glaring at me in the other seven monitors. Oh no! Look behind you, Omega, you fool! Treachery! There's someone sneaking out of the girl's room. He's got a gun. No, not a gun. A CO_2 dart pistol!

"Spit!" Oh, no, Omega's been hit in the back of the neck. He's rolling down the stairs, out cold. What is going on here?

Oh my wicked Master! Two men are handcuffing Omega at the bottom of the steps. Four boys and a girl are racing up the stairs with flashlights, yelling and screaming at the top of their lungs, "Praise the Lord! We did it! Thank you, Jesus!" They're embracing the man with the tranquilizer gun.

I think I'm going to be ill. It's your enemy, the other three boys and the little girl. How in the world . . . ¿

Dummies! We've been deceived by a bunch of dummies! Who¿ How¿ Oh, Spitwad. The man with the CO_2 gun . . . I know him. He goes to the Lighthouse. FBI.

I'm hanging up, Spitwad. I've got a superiorly splitting migraine. Oh, wouldn't you know it . . . I think I'm out of aspirin.

What happened?

To most worthless and unemployed Spitwad,

I t was all a blasted trap. A reverse trap sprung on the hunter. That vile Light-lover FBI agent received a tip from an informant on the coast telling him that a top-level assassin was on the move, headed for his city. From there it had been a simple matter of following him and then bugging his motel room when he stepped out to purchase a few items.

Why didn't *our* FBI friends in high places put a stop to this meddling with our affairs? No doubt there was some serious interference going on by way of the Adversary. Our Most Angry Master Below is demanding a full explanation. He will not get one. He never does.

When the Christian agent and his team tapped the over-confident assassin's phone, the connection with Leaven was easily established. A quick phone call was made by Omega, an address was given to him—your enemy's—and directions to the pick-up spot for the payoff was provided.

That was all the FBI needed. Omega should have not been so careless. He should have used a public phone. He should never have been so cocky as to be contacted in his room. Any fool knows that. But Leaven was so confident that the execution had been set up flawlessly . . . pride goeth before a fall. . . .

When your enemy's parents were given the weekend vacation, the agents then knew the time-frame during which the assassin would strike. From then on it was just a waiting game.

The four boy Light-lovers and the Light-girl were placed under heavily armed guard in the basement. The basement windows had been boarded up ahead of time and reinforced on the inside with steel, thus forcing the assassin to enter the house via the first floor. Their precautions also successfully hid their basement hideout from prying eyes.

The FBI thugs had set-up shop in the basement Thursday night, sneaking in under the cover of darkness.

There were no visible movements on their part after midnight on Thursday. They knew that the assassin would be in the area by then, watching the house and neighborhood like a hawk.

Omega had seen the jock and jockling arrive and your enemy's parents leave early Friday evening. A telephone repair truck on the street had been his cover.

It's all that cursed prayer power, Spitwad. Our eyes were simply blinded to it all. Even Eclipse was taken totally off-guard.

The only thing that gives me hope is to realize

how seldom the Light-soldiers ever mount a serious movement of prayer. The lazy saints tire so easily, grumbling and complaining that prayer is too hard.

Of course we are the ones that make prayer so difficult for them, fighting tooth-and-nail every step of the way. They don't understand that we are fighting for our own wretched lives!

Well, back to the wrap-up, Spitwad. Other FBI agents were lurking in the wooded shadows at the rendezvous point. They caught the messenger easily. He was expecting a smooth drop-off and information exchange and practically soiled his pants when he was surrounded by four agents with handguns pointed at his forehead.

The worthless dupe couldn't have been more cooperative with the authorities. I can't imagine why.

Leaven did manage to do one thing right. The messenger had been instructed to call a special untraceable phone number precisely at 2 o'clock and leave a coded message if all had gone according to plan. Having been detained by the government killjoys for a crucial four minutes, he proceeded to drive back toward the Leaven hideout.

The agents followed at a safe distance, figuring they were closing in on the biggest bust of their careers. They were, but not in the way they expected.

The messenger, so upset by the turn of events, forgot to make his 2 o'clock phone call. Still over four miles from the Leaven meeting, at precisely 2:05 A.M., his car exploded into flames.

And so, Leaven lives on. But not in your old hometown. Personally, I don't believe that a certain mayor, police chief, or outspoken talk show host are long for this world. Too risky.

But not to worry, Leaven has others who will soon take their places. We can only hope they will not be so careless.

If the FBI moves in quickly enough, things could get very interesting around here in the days to come. To be honest, I would relish seeing that egomaniac, Eclipse, sweat it out a bit.

The assassin himself may try a plea bargain, but he is a fool if he talks. A dead fool. Leaven holds a very dim view of failure.

Of course, the nabbing of such a top-level assassin as Omega has made the Light-lovers instant heroes at their high school. The boldness in their witness to their friends right now is frightening.

And prayer at the Lighthouse continues. The blond strengthens with each passing day. And it seems like the scandal of the youth pastor has been all but forgotten.

The fickle public has a short memory. Even excitement over current events like foiled assassinations passes quickly.

We will soon be able to get back to business again. Or should I say, *somebody* will be able to get back to business soon. But not you and I, Spacebrain.

I fear that my life is to be forever cursed with your irritating presence. . . . We have been given new orders.

252

We are expected in Bangkok by nightfall, Thailand time. Oh, how I hate the tropics!

Your superior on welfare,

Slimeball

Steps to Freedom in Christ

Freedom *in Christ* is having the desire and power to do God's will. Being free in Christ means being released from the chains of sins from our past, problems in the present and fears of the future. It is not a life of perfection, but progress! All these qualities may not be yours now, but *they are meant for everyone who is in Christ.*

If you have received Christ as your Savior, He has already set you free through His victory over sin on the cross and His resurrection. It is your responsibility, as one who knows Christ, to do whatever is needed to have a right relationship with God. Your eternal life is not at stake; you are safe and secure in Christ. But you will not experience all that Christ has for you if you don't understand who you are in Christ and don't know how to live according to that truth.

We've got great news for you! You are not a helpless victim caught between two nearly-equal-but-opposite heavenly superpowers—God and Satan. Satan is a deceiver. Only God is all-powerful, always present, and all-knowing. Sometimes sin and the presence of evil may seem more real than the presence of God, but that's part of Satan's tricky lie. *Satan is a defeated enemy,* and you are *in Christ,* the victor.

The battle is for your mind. "This isn't going to work" or "God doesn't love me" are lies implanted in your mind by deceiving spirits. If you believe them, you will have a difficult time working through these steps. Those thoughts can control you only if you believe them. If you are working through these steps by yourself, don't pay attention to any lying or threatening thoughts in your mind. If you're working through them with a trusted friend, youth pastor, parent or counselor (which we strongly recommend), share with them any thoughts you are having that are in opposition to what you are trying to do. As soon as you uncover the lie and choose to believe the truth, the power of Satan is broken.

As believers in Christ, we can pray with authority to stop any interference by Satan. Here is a prayer and declaration to get you started. Read them (and all prayers and declarations in these steps) out loud.

Prayer

Dear Heavenly Father, I know that You are always here and present in my life. You are the only all-knowing, all-powerful, ever-present God. I desperately need You, because without You I can do nothing. I believe the Bible because it tells me what is really true. I refuse to believe the lies of Satan. I stand in the truth that all authority in heaven and on earth has been given to the resurrected Christ. I ask You to protect my thoughts and mind and lead me into all truth. I choose to submit to the Holy Spirit. Please reveal to my mind everything that You want to teach me today. I ask for and trust in Your wisdom. I pray for Your complete protection over me. In Jesus' name. Amen.

Declaration

In the name and the authority of the Lord Jesus Christ, I command Satan and all evil spirits to let go of me so that I can be free to know and choose to do the will of God. As a child of God, seated with Christ in the heavenlies, I pray that every enemy of the Lord Jesus

Christ be bound and gagged to silence. I say to Satan and all of his evil workers, "You cannot inflict any pain or in any way stop or hinder God's will from being done today in my life."

As you go through these *Steps to Freedom in Christ*, remember that Satan cannot read your mind, so he won't obey your thoughts. Only God knows what you are thinking. As you go through each step, it is important that you submit to God inwardly and resist the devil by reading *out loud* each prayer.

May the Lord greatly touch your life during this time. He will give you the strength to make it through. It is essential that you work through *all* seven steps, so don't allow yourself to become discouraged and give up. Remember, the freedom that Christ purchased for all believers on the cross is meant for *you!*

Step 1:
Counterfeit Versus Real

The first step toward experiencing your freedom in Christ is to renounce (to reject and turn your back on all past, present and future involvement with) any participation in Satan-inspired occult practices, things done in secret and involvement in non-Christian religions. You must renounce any activity and group which denies Jesus Christ, offers direction through any source other than the absolute authority of the written Word of God, or requires secret initiations, ceremonies, promises or pacts (covenants). Begin with the following prayer:

Dear Heavenly Father, I ask You to reveal to me anything that I have done or that someone has done to me that is

257

spiritually wrong. Reveal to my mind any and all involvement I have knowingly or unknowingly had with cult or occult practices or false teachers. I want to experience Your freedom and do Your will. I ask this in Jesus' name. Amen.

Even if you took part in something as a game or as a joke, you need to renounce it. We need to realize that Satan will try to take advantage of anything he can in our lives. Even if you were just standing by and watching others do it, you need to renounce it. Even if you did it just once and had no idea it was evil, you still need to renounce it. Make sure you remove any and every possible foothold for Satan in your life. Use the following checklist as your guide.

Non-Christian Spiritual Checklist
(check all activities that apply to you)

❏ Out of body experience (astral projection)
❏ Ouija board
❏ Bloody Mary
❏ Light as a feather (or other occult games)
❏ Table lifting or body lifting
❏ Magic Eight Ball
❏ Using spells or curses
❏ Attempting to control others by putting thoughts in their heads
❏ Automatic writing
❏ Spirit guides
❏ Fortune-telling
❏ Tarot cards
❏ Palm reading
❏ Astrology/horoscopes
❏ Hypnosis
❏ Seances
❏ Black or white magic
❏ Dungeons and Dragons (or other fantasy role-playing games)
❏ Video or computer games involving occult powers or cruel violence
❏ Blood pacts or cutting yourself on purpose
❏ Objects of worship/ crystals/good-luck charms

- ☐ Sexual spirits
- ☐ Martial arts (involving Eastern mysticism, meditation or devotion to sensei)
- ☐ Buddhism (including Zen)
- ☐ Rosicrucianism
- ☐ Hinduism
- ☐ Mormonism (Latter-day Saints)
- ☐ Jehovah Witness
- ☐ New Age philosophy
- ☐ New Age medicine
- ☐ Masonry
- ☐ Christian Science
- ☐ Science of Creative Intelligence
- ☐ The Way International
- ☐ Unification Church (Moonies)
- ☐ The Forum (est)
- ☐ Church of the Living Word
- ☐ Children of God (Children of Love)
- ☐ Worldwide Church of God (Armstrong)
- ☐ Scientology
- ☐ Unitarianism
- ☐ Roy Masters
- ☐ Silva Mind Control
- ☐ Transcendental Meditation (TM)
- ☐ Yoga
- ☐ Hare Krishna
- ☐ Bahaism
- ☐ Native American spirit worship
- ☐ Idolization of rock stars, actors/actresses, sports heroes, etc.
- ☐ Islam
- ☐ Black Muslim

Note: This is not a complete list. If you have any doubts about an activity not included, renounce your involvement in it. If it has come to mind here, trust that the Lord wants you to renounce it.

Anti-Christian movies (be specific as you renounce them)

Anti-Christian music (be specific as you renounce them)

Anti-Christian TV shows or video games (be specific)

Anti-Christian books, magazines and comics (be specific)

1. Have you ever heard or seen a spiritual being in your room?

2. Have you had an imaginary friend that talked to you?

3. Have you ever heard voices in your head or had repeating, nagging thoughts such as "I'm dumb," "I'm ugly," "Nobody loves me," "I can't do anything right"—like there was a conversation going on in your head? Explain.

4. Have you or anyone in your family ever consulted a medium, spiritist or channeler?

5. What other spiritual experiences have you had that would be considered out of the ordinary (telepathy,

speaking in a trance, supernatural knowledge, contact with aliens, etc.)?

6. Have you ever been involved in satanic worship of any kind or attended a concert in which Satan was the focus?

7. Have you ever made a vow or pact?

Once you have completed the checklist, confess and renounce each item you were involved in by praying aloud the following prayer. (Repeat the prayer separately for each item on your list.)

Lord, I confess that I have participated in _____. I thank You for Your forgiveness and I renounce any and all involvement with _____.

Step 2:
Deception Versus Truth

God's Word is true, and we need to accept the truth deep in our hearts (Psalm 51:6). When King David lived a lie, he really suffered. When he finally found freedom by admitting that he had sinned, he wrote, "How blessed is the man . . . in whose spirit there is no deceit!" (Psalm 32:2). We must stop lying to ourselves and to each other and speak the truth in love (Ephesians 4:15,25).

Start this important step by praying the following prayer out loud.

Dear Heavenly Father, I know that You want me to face the truth and that I must be honest with You. I know that choosing to believe the truth will set me free. I have been deceived by Satan, the father of lies, and I have deceived myself as well. I thought I could hide from You, but You see everything and still love me. I pray in the name of the Lord Jesus Christ, asking You to rebuke all of Satan's demons through Him who shed His blood and rose from the dead for me.

I trust in Jesus alone to save me, and so I am Your child. Therefore, by the authority of the Lord Jesus Christ, I command all evil spirits to leave my presence. I ask the Holy Spirit to lead me into all truth. I ask You, Father, to look deep inside me and know my heart. Show me if there is anything in me that I am trying to hide, because I want to be free. In Jesus' name. Amen.

It is important to know that, in addition to false teachers and deceiving spirits, you can fool yourself. Now that you are alive in Christ and forgiven, you don't need to live a lie or defend yourself like you used to. Christ is now your truth and defense.

Ways you can deceive yourself (check the ones that are true of you):

- ☐ Hearing God's Word but not doing it (James 1:22; 4:17)
- ☐ Saying I have no sin (1 John 1:8)
- ☐ Thinking I am something I'm really not (Galatians 6:3)
- ☐ Thinking I am wise in the things of the world (1 Corinthians 3:18,19)
- ☐ Thinking I will not reap what I sow (Galatians 6:7)
- ☐ Thinking that ungodly people will share in God's kingdom (1 Corinthians 6:9)
- ☐ Thinking that I can hang out with bad people and they won't have any bad influence on me (1 Corinthians 15:33)
- ☐ Thinking I can be a good Christian and still do and say what I want even if it hurts people (James 1:22)

Use the following prayer of confession for each item that you have checked. Pray for each item separately.

Lord, I confess that I have deceived myself by _____. I thank You for Your forgiveness and commit myself to believing Your truth.

Wrong ways of defending yourself (check the ones that you have participated in):
- ☐ Refusing to face the bad things that have happened to me
- ☐ Escaping from the real world by daydreaming, TV, movies, computer or video games, music, etc.
- ☐ Withdrawing from people to avoid rejection
- ☐ Going back to a less threatening time of life
- ☐ Taking out frustrations on others
- ☐ Blaming others for my problems
- ☐ Making excuses for poor behavior

Use the following prayer of confession for each item that you participated in. Pray through each item separately.

Lord, I confess that I have defended myself wrongly by _____. I thank You for Your forgiveness and commit myself to trusting in You to defend and protect me.

The Christian needs only one defense—Jesus. Knowing that you are completely forgiven and accepted as God's child sets you free to face reality and declare your total dependence upon Him.

The New Age movement twists the truth by saying we create reality through what we believe. We can't create reality. We *face* reality with our minds. Simply having faith is not the key issue here. It's what or who you believe in that makes the difference. If what you believe is not true, then how you live will not be right. Ask yourself, "Is the object of my faith trustworthy?"

Faith is something you decide to do, whether or not you feel like doing it. Just believing doesn't make it true. Instead we know *it's true, therefore we believe it.*

Read aloud the following statement of truth, thinking about the words as you read them. This will help you renew your mind and replace any lies you have believed with the truth.

Statement of Truth

1. I believe that there is only one true and living God (Exodus 20:2,3) who is the Father, Son and Holy Spirit. He is worthy of all honor, praise, and glory. I believe that He made all things and holds all things together (Colossians 1:16,17).

2. I recognize Jesus Christ as the Messiah, the Word who became flesh and lived with us (John 1:1,14). I believe that He came to destroy the works of the devil (1 John 3:8).

3. I believe that God showed how much he loves me by having Jesus die for me, even though I was sinful (Romans 5:8). I believe that God rescued me from the dark power of Satan and brought me into the kingdom of His Son, who forgives my sins and sets me free (Colossians 1:13,14).

4. I believe I am spiritually strong because Jesus is my strength. I have authority to stand against Satan because I am God's child (1 John 3:1-3). I believe that I was saved by the grace of God through faith, that it was a gift and not the result of any works of mine (Ephesians 2:8,9).

5. I choose to be strong in the Lord and in the strength of His might (Ephesians 6:10). I put no confidence in the

flesh (Philippians 3:3) because my weapons of spiritual battle are not of the flesh. But they are powerful through God for the tearing down of Satan's strongholds (2 Corinthians 10:4). I put on the whole armor of God (Ephesians 6:10-20), and I resolve to stand firm in my faith and resist the evil one (1 Peter 5:8,9).

6. I believe that apart from Christ I can do nothing (John 15:5), yet I can do all things through Him who strengthens me (Philippians 4:13). Therefore, I choose to rely totally on Christ. I choose to abide in Christ in order to bear much fruit and glorify the Lord (John 15:8). I announce to Satan that Jesus is my Lord (1 Corinthians 12:30), and I reject any counterfeit gifts or works of Satan in my life.

7. I believe that the truth will set me free (John 8:32). I stand against Satan's lies by taking every thought captive in obedience to Christ (2 Corinthians 10:5). I believe that the Bible is the only reliable guide for my life (2 Timothy 3:15,16). I choose to speak the truth in love (Ephesians 4:15).

8. I choose to present my body to God as an instrument of righteousness, a living and holy sacrifice, and to renew my mind with God's Word (Romans 6:13; 12:1,2). I put off the old self with its evil practices and put on the new self (Colossians 3:9,10). I am a new creation in Christ (2 Corinthians 5:17).

9. I ask my Heavenly Father to direct my life and give me power to live by the Holy Spirit (Ephesians 5:18), so that He can guide me into all truth (John 16:13). He will give me strength to live above sin and not carry out the desires of my flesh. I crucify the flesh and choose to be led by the Holy Spirit and obey Him (Galatians 5:16,24).

10. I renounce all selfish goals and choose the greatest goal of love (1 Timothy 1:5). I choose to obey the two greatest

commandments: to love the Lord my God with all my heart, soul and mind, and to love my neighbor as myself (Matthew 22:37-39).

11. I believe that Jesus has all authority in heaven and on earth (Matthew 28:18) and that He rules over everything (Colossians 2:10). I believe that Satan and his demons have been defeated by Christ and are subject to me since I am a member of Christ's body (Ephesians 1:19,20; 2:6). So, I obey the command to submit to God and to resist the devil (James 4:7), and I command Satan, by the authority of the Lord Jesus Christ, to leave my presence.

Step 3:
Bitterness Versus Forgiveness

When you do not forgive those who hurt you, you become a wide-open target for Satan. God commands us to forgive others as we have been forgiven (Ephesians 4:31). You need to obey this command so that Satan can't take advantage of you (2 Corinthians 2:11). Ask God to bring to your mind the names of those people you need to forgive by praying the following prayer out loud. (Remember to let this prayer come from your heart as well as your mouth!)

Dear Heavenly Father, I thank You for Your great kindness and patience. I know that Your kindness has led me to turn from my sins (Romans 2:4). I know that I have not been completely kind, patient and loving toward those who have hurt me. I have had bad thoughts and feelings toward them. I ask You to bring to my mind all the people that I need to forgive (Matthew 18:35). I ask You to bring to the surface all my painful memories so that I can choose to forgive these

266

people from my heart. I pray this in the precious name of Jesus, who has forgiven me and who will heal my hurts. Amen.

On a sheet of paper, make a list of the names of people who come to your mind. At this point, don't question whether you need to forgive them or not. If a name comes to your mind, write it down.

After God's Spirit finishes the list, write "me" at the bottom. Forgiving yourself means accepting God's cleansing and forgiveness. Also write "thoughts against God." It is very common to harbor angry thoughts toward God, though we don't actually need to forgive Him because He is perfect. Sometimes, however, we expect or even demand that God act in a certain way in our lives. When He doesn't do what we want in the way we want, we can get angry. Those feelings can become a wall between us and God, and so we must let them go.

Before you begin working through the process of forgiving the people on your list, stop and consider what real forgiveness is and what it is not.

Forgiveness is not forgetting. People who want to forget all their pain before they get around to forgiving someone, usually find they cannot. God commands us to forgive now. You may not be able to forget your past, but you can be free from it by forgiving others. When we bring up the past and use it against others, we are showing that we have not yet forgiven them (Mark 11:25,26).

Forgiveness is a choice, a decision of the will. Since God requires us to forgive, it is something we can do. Forgiveness seems hard because it pulls against our sense of what is right and fair. We naturally want revenge for the things we have suffered. But we are told by God never to take our own revenge (Romans 12:19). You might think, "Why should I let him off the hook?" That is exactly the problem! As long as you do not forgive, you are still hooked to those who hurt you! You are still chained to your past. By forgiving, you let them off *your* hook, but they are not off *God's* hook. We must trust Him to deal with the other person justly, fairly and mercifully, something we cannot do.

Forgiveness is agreeing to live with the consequences of another person's sin. Forgiveness costs you something. You choose to pay the price for the evil you forgive. But you are going to live with the consequences whether you want to or not. Your only choice is whether you will do so in the bondage of bitterness or in the freedom of forgiveness.

How do you forgive from your heart? You allow God to bring to the surface your mental agony, emotional pain and feelings of hurt toward those who hurt you. If your forgiveness doesn't bring out or reach down to the emotional core of your life, it will be incomplete. Too often we try to bury the pain deep inside us, making it hard to get in touch with how we really feel. Though we may not know how to—or even want to—bring our feelings to the surface, God does. Let Him bring the pain to the surface so that He can deal with it. This is where God's gentle healing process begins.

Don't wait to forgive until you feel like forgiving. You will never get there. Your emotions will begin to heal once you obey God's command to forgive. Satan will have lost his power over you in that area and God's healing touch will take over. For now, it is freedom that will be gained, not necessarily a feeling.

As you pray, God may bring to mind painful memories that you have totally forgotten. Let Him do this, even if it hurts. God wants you to be free; forgiving these people is the only way. Don't try to excuse the offender's behavior, even if it is someone close to you.

It's time to begin. For each person on your list, pray aloud:

Lord, I forgive _____ for _____ even though it made me feel _____.

Once you have dealt with every offense that has come to your mind, and you have honestly expressed how that person hurt you, conclude by forgiving him or her.

Lord, I choose not to hold any of these things against _____ any longer. I thank You for setting me free from the bondage of my bitterness toward _____. I choose now to ask You to bless _____. In Jesus' name. Amen.

Step 4:
Rebellion Versus Submission

We live in rebellious times. Often people don't respect people in the positions of authority that God has placed over them. They have problems with living in submission to them. You can easily be deceived into thinking that those in authority over you are robbing you of your freedom. In reality, however, God has placed them there for your protection.

Rebelling against God and His authorities is serious business. It gives Satan an opportunity to attack you. Submission is the only solution. God requires more of you, however, than just the outward appearance of submission. He wants you to sincerely submit to your authorities (especially your parents) from the heart.

The Bible makes it clear that we have two main responsibilities toward those in authority over us: to pray for them and submit to them. Pray the following prayer out loud from your heart.

Dear Heavenly Father, You have said in the Bible that rebellion is the same thing as witchcraft, and being self-willed is like serving false gods (1 Samuel 15:23). I know that I have disobeyed and rebelled in my heart against You and those You have placed in authority over me. I thank You for Your forgiveness for my rebellion. By the shed blood of the Lord Jesus Christ, I pray that all doors that I opened to evil spirits through my rebellion would now be closed. I pray that You will show me all the ways I have been rebellious. I choose to adopt a submissive spirit and servant's heart. In Jesus' precious name I pray, Amen.

Being under authority is an act of faith! By submitting, you are trusting God to work through His lines of authority.

There may be times when parents, teachers, etc., abuse their authority and break the laws which are ordained by God for the protection of innocent people. In those cases, you need to seek help from a higher authority for your protection. The laws in your state may require that such abuse be reported to the police or other protective agencies.

If authorities abuse their position by clearly asking you to break God's law or compromise your commitment to Him, you need to obey God rather than man. We are all told to submit to one another in the fear of Christ (Ephesians 5:21). In addition, however, God uses specific lines of authority to protect us and give order to our daily lives.

- ☐ Civil government (traffic laws, drinking laws, etc.): Romans 13:1-7; 1 Timothy 2:2; 1 Peter 2:13-17
- ☐ Parents, stepparents or legal guardians: Ephesians 6:1,2

❑ Teachers, coaches, and school officials: Romans 13:1-4
❑ Your boss: 1 Peter 2:18
❑ Church leaders (pastor, youth pastor, Sunday school teacher): Hebrews 13:17
❑ God Himself: Daniel 9:5,9

Examine each of the six areas of authority listed above and ask the Lord to forgive you for those times you have not respected the position or been submissive to the people over you by praying:

Lord, I agree with You that I have been rebellious toward _____. Please forgive me for this rebellion. I choose to be submissive and obedient to Your Word. In Jesus' name. Amen.

Step 5:
Pride Versus Humility

Pride is a killer. Pride says, "I can do it! I can get myself out of this mess without God or anyone else's help." Oh no, we can't! We absolutely need God, and we desperately need each other. Paul wrote, "We...worship in the Spirit of God and glory in Christ Jesus and put no confidence in the flesh" (Philippians 3:3).

Humility is confidence properly placed in God. We are to be "strong in the Lord, and in the strength of His might" (Ephesians 6:10). James 4:5-10 and 1 Peter 5:1-10 tell us that spiritual problems will flow when we are proud. Use the following prayer to express your commitment to live humbly before God.

Dear Heavenly Father, You have said that pride goes before destruction and an arrogant spirit before stumbling (Proverbs

16:18). I confess that I have been thinking mainly of myself and not of others. I have not denied myself, picked up my cross daily and followed You (Matthew 16:24). In so doing, I have given ground to the enemy in my life. I have believed that I could be successful by living according to my own power and resources. I now confess that I have sinned against You by placing my will before Yours and by centering my life around myself instead of You. I renounce my pride and my selfishness and, by so doing, close any doors I opened in my life to the enemies of the Lord Jesus Christ. I choose to rely on the Holy Spirit's power and guidance so that I can do Your will. I give my heart to You and stand against all the ways that Satan attacks me. I ask You to show me how to live for others. I now choose to make others more important than myself and to make You the most important of all (Romans 12:10; Matthew 6:33). Please show me now specific ways in which I have lived pridefully. I ask this in the name of my Lord Jesus Christ. Amen.

Having made that commitment in prayer, allow God to show you any specific areas of your life where you have been prideful, such as:

- ❏ I have a stronger desire to do my will than God's will.
- ❏ I rely on my own strengths and abilities rather than God's.
- ❏ Too often I think my ideas are better than other people's ideas.
- ❏ I want to control how others act rather than develop self-control.
- ❏ I sometimes consider myself more important than others.
- ❏ I have a tendency to think I don't need other people.
- ❏ I find it difficult to admit when I am wrong.

☐ I tend to be a people-pleaser instead of a God-pleaser.

☐ I am overly concerned about getting credit for doing good things.

☐ I often think I am more humble than others.

☐ I often feel my needs are more important than others' needs.

☐ I consider myself better than others because of my academic, artistic or athletic abilities and accomplishments.

Remember to include other areas God points out to you. Then, for each of the above areas that has been true in your life, pray out loud:

Lord, I agree I have been prideful in the area of _____. Thank You for forgiving me for this pridefulness. I choose to humble myself and place all my confidence in You. Amen.

Step 6:
Bondage Versus Freedom

The next step to freedom deals with the sins that have become habits in your life. Teens who have been caught in the vicious cycle of "sin-confess-sin-confess" need to realize that the road to victory is "sin-confess-*resist*" (James 4:7). Breaking habitual sin often requires help from a trusted brother or sister in Christ. James 5:16 says, "Confess your sins to one another, and pray for one another, so that you may be healed. The effective prayer of a righteous man can accomplish much." Seek out a stronger Christian who will lift you up in prayer and hold you accountable in your areas of weakness.

Sometimes the assurance of 1 John 1:9 is sufficient: "If we confess our sins, He is faithful and righteous to forgive us our sins and to cleanse us from all unrighteousness."

Remember, confession is not saying "I'm sorry"; it's openly admitting, "I did it." Whether you need the help of others or just the accountability of God, pray the following prayer out loud:

Dear Heavenly Father, You have told us to "put on the Lord Jesus Christ, and make no provision for the flesh in regard to this lust" (Romans 13:14). I agree that I have given in to fleshly lusts which wage war against my soul (1 Peter 2:11). I thank You that in Christ my sins are forgiven; but I have broken Your holy law and given the devil an opportunity to wage war in my body (Romans 6:12,13; James 4:1; 1 Peter 5:8). I come before Your presence now to admit these sins and to seek Your cleansing (1 John 1:9) that I may be freed from the bondage of sin. I now ask You to reveal to my mind the ways that I have broken Your moral law and grieved the Holy Spirit. In Jesus' precious name I pray. Amen.

There are many sins that can control us. Look through the following list and ask the Holy Spirit to reveal to your mind which of these you need to resolve. Then pray the following prayer for each area.

- ❑ stealing
- ❑ lying
- ❑ fighting
- ❑ hatred
- ❑ jealousy, envy
- ❑ anger
- ❑ complaining and criticism
- ❑ impure thoughts
- ❑ eagerness for lustful pleasure
- ❑ perfectionism
- ❑ cheating
- ❑ gossiping
- ❑ procrastination (putting things off)
- ❑ swearing
- ❑ greed/materialism
- ❑ apathy/laziness
- ❑ other

Lord, I admit that I have committed the sin of _____. I thank You for Your forgiveness and cleansing. I turn away from this sin and turn to You, Lord. Strengthen me by Your Holy Spirit to obey You. In Jesus' name. Amen.

It is our responsibility not to allow sin to have control over our bodies. We must not use our bodies or someone else's as an instrument of unrighteousness (Romans 6:12,13). If you are struggling with sexual sins (pornography, masturbation, heavy petting, heavy kissing, oral sex, sexual intercourse) pray as follows:

Lord, I ask You to reveal to my mind every sexual use of my body as an instrument of unrighteousness. In Jesus' precious name I pray. Amen.

As the Lord brings to your mind every sexual use of your body, whether it was done to you (rape, incest, sexual molestation) or willingly by you, renounce every occasion.

Lord, I renounce (name the specific use of your body) with (name the person involved) and I ask You to break that sinful bond between us.

After you have completed the above exercises, commit your body to the Lord by praying out loud from your heart:

Lord, I renounce all these uses of my body as an instrument of unrighteousness, and I admit my willful participation. Lord, I choose to present my eyes, my mouth, my mind, my hands and feet—my whole body to You as instruments of righteousness. I now present my body to You as a living sacrifice, holy and acceptable to You, and I choose to reserve the sexual use of my body for marriage only (Hebrews 13:4).

I reject the lie of Satan that my body is not clean or that it is dirty or in any way unacceptable to You as a result of my past sexual experiences. Lord, I thank You that You have totally cleansed and forgiven me, and that You love me just as I am. Therefore, I can accept myself and my body as cleansed in Your eyes. In Jesus' name. Amen.

Special Prayers for Specific Needs

Homosexuality

Lord, I renounce the lie that You have created me or anyone else to be homosexual, and I agree that You clearly forbid homosexual behavior. I accept myself as a child of God and declare that You created me a man (or a woman). I renounce all homosexual thoughts, urges or drives, as well as any bondage of Satan, that have perverted my relationships with others. I announce that I am free to relate to the opposite sex and my own sex in the way that You intended. In Jesus' name. Amen.

Abortion

Lord, I confess that I was not a proper guardian and keeper of the life You entrusted to me, and I ask your forgiveness. I choose to accept your forgiveness by forgiving myself, and I now commit that child to You for Your care for all eternity. In Jesus' name. Amen.

Suicidal Tendencies

I renounce suicidal thoughts and any attempts I may have made to take my own life. I renounce the lie that life is hopeless and that I can find peace and freedom by taking my own life. Satan is a thief, and he desires to steal, kill and destroy. I choose life in Christ, who said He came to give me life and to give it to the full. I choose to accept Your forgiveness by forgiving myself, and I choose to believe that there is always hope in Christ. In Jesus' name. Amen.

Eating Disorders or Cutting Yourself

I renounce the lie that my value as a person is dependent upon my physical beauty, my weight or size. I renounce cutting myself, vomiting, or using laxatives, or starving myself as a means of cleansing myself of evil or altering my appearance. I announce that only the blood of the Lord Jesus Christ cleanses me from sin. I accept the reality that there may be sin present in me due to the lies I have believed and the wrongful use of my body. But I renounce the lie that I am evil or that any part of my body is evil. My body is the temple of the Holy Spirit and I belong to God. I am totally accepted by God in Christ, just as I am. In Jesus' name. Amen.

Substance Abuse

Lord, I confess that I have misused substances (alcohol, tobacco, food, prescription or street drugs) for the purpose of pleasure, to escape reality, or to cope with difficult problems. I confess that I have abused my body and programmed my mind in a harmful way. I have not allowed Your Holy Spirit to guide me. I ask Your forgiveness, and I reject any satanic connection or influence in my life due to my misuse of drugs or food. I cast my cares onto Christ who loves me, and I commit myself to no longer give in to substance abuse, but instead to allow the Holy Spirit to lead and empower me. In Jesus' name. Amen.

After you have confessed all known sin, pray:

I now confess these sins to You and claim, through the blood of the Lord Jesus Christ, my forgiveness and cleansing. I cancel all grounds that evil spirits have gained through my willful involvement in sin. I ask this in the wonderful name of my Lord and Savior, Jesus Christ. Amen.

Step 7:
Curses Versus Blessings

The last step to freedom is to renounce the sins of your ancestors and any curses which may have been placed on you. In giving the Ten Commandments, God said, "You shall not make yourselves any idols: any images resembling animals, birds, or fish. You must never bow to an image or worship it in any way; for I, the Lord your God, am very possessive. I will not share your affection with any other god! And when I punish people for their sins, the punishment continues upon the children, grandchildren, and great-grandchildren of those who hate me" (Exodus 20:4,5 TLB).

Demonic or familiar spirits can be passed on from one generation to the next, if you don't renounce the sins of your ancestors and claim your new spiritual heritage in Christ. You are not guilty of the sin of any ancestor, but because of their sin, Satan has gained access to your family.

In order to walk free from the sins of your ancestors and any demonic influences, read the following declaration and pray the following prayer out loud. Let the words come from your heart as you remember the authority you have in Christ Jesus.

Declaration

I reject and disown all the sins of my ancestors. As one who has been delivered from the domain of darkness into the kingdom of God's Son, I cancel all demonic working that has been passed down to me from my family. As one who has been crucified and raised with Jesus Christ and who sits with Him in heavenly places, I renounce all satanic assignments that are directed toward me. I cancel every curse that Satan and his workers have put on me. I announce to Satan and all his forces that Christ redeemed me from the curse of the Law, having become a curse for me (Galatians 3:13) when He died for my sins on the cross. I reject any and every way that Satan may claim ownership of me. I belong to the Lord Jesus Christ who purchased me with His own blood. I reject all the blood sacrifices in which Satan may claim ownership of me. I declare myself to be eternally and completely signed over and committed to the Lord Jesus Christ. By the authority that I have in Jesus Christ, I command every familiar spirit and every enemy of the Lord Jesus Christ that is influencing me, to leave my presence. I commit myself to my Heavenly Father, to do His will from this day forward.

Prayer

Dear Heavenly Father, I come to You as Your child, purchased by the blood of the Lord Jesus Christ. You are the Lord of the universe and the Lord of my life. I submit my body to You as an instrument of righteousness, a living sacrifice, that I may glorify You in my body. I now ask Your Holy Spirit to lead and empower me to know and do Your will. I commit myself to the renewing of my mind in order to prove that Your will is good, perfect and acceptable for me. All this I do in the name and authority of the Lord Jesus Christ. Amen.

Maintaining Freedom

Freedom must be maintained. We cannot emphasize that point enough. You have won a very important battle in an ongoing war. Freedom will remain yours as long as you keep choosing truth and standing firm in the strength of the Lord. If new memories should surface or if you become aware of lies that you have believed or other non-Christian experiences you have had, renounce them and choose the truth. If you realize that there are some other people you need to forgive, Step 3 will remind you what to do. Some people have found it helpful to walk through the *Steps to Freedom in Christ* again. As you do, read the instructions carefully.

We recommend that you read the books *Stomping Out the Darkness* and the *Bondage Breaker Youth Edition*. To maintain your freedom, we strongly suggest the following as well.

1. Get involved in a loving church youth group or Bible study where you can be open and honest with other believers your age.
2. Study your Bible daily. There are many great teen Bibles around for you to use. Begin to get into God's Word and memorize key verses. Remember it is the *truth that sets you free* and it is *truth that keeps you free!*
3. Learn to take every thought captive to the obedience of Christ. Assume responsibility for your thought life. Don't let your mind go passive. Reject all lies, choose to focus on the truth, and stand firm in your identity in Christ.

4. Don't drift away! It is very easy to become lazy in your thoughts and slip back into old patterns of thinking. Share your struggles openly with a trusted friend who will pray for you.
5. Don't expect others to fight your battles for you. They can't and they won't. Others can encourage you, but they can't think, pray, read the Bible or choose the truth for you.
6. Commit yourself to daily prayer. Prayer is dependence upon God.

For more information about Freedom in Christ
Youth Ministries or the resources they have to
offer, please write or call:

Freedom in Christ
Youth Ministries
491 E. Lambert Road
La Habra, CA 90631
Phone: (310) 691-9128

Freedom in Christ Ministries

Purpose: *Freedom in Christ Ministries is an interdenomiational, international, Bible-teaching Church ministry which exists to glorify God by equipping churches and mission groups, enabling them to fulfill their mission of establishing people free in Christ.*

Freedom in Christ Ministries offers a number of valuable video, audio, and print resources that will help both those in need and those who counsel. Among the topics covered are:

Resolving Personal Conflicts

Search for Identity ■ *Walking by Faith* ■ *Faith Renewal* ■ *Renewing the Mind* ■ *Battle for the Mind* ■ *Emotions* ■ *Relationships* ■ *Forgiveness*

Resolving Spiritual Conflicts

Position of Believer ■ *Authority* ■ *Protection* ■ *Vulnerability* ■ *Temptation* ■ *Accusation* ■ *Deception & Discernment* ■ *Steps to Freedom*

Spiritual Conflicts and Biblical Counseling

Biblical Integration ■ *Theological Basis* ■ *Walking by the Spirit* ■ *Surviving the Crisis* ■ *The Process of Growth* ■ *Counseling and Christ* ■ *Counseling the Spiritually Afflicted* ■ *Ritual Abuse*

The Seduction of Our Children

God's Answer ■ *Identity and Self-Worth* ■ *Styles of Communication* ■ *Discipline* ■ *Spiritual Conflicts and Prayer* ■ *Steps to Freedom*

Resolving Spiritual Conflicts and Cross-Cultural Ministry
Dr. Timothy Warner

Worldview Problems ■ *Warfare Relationships* ■ *Christians and Demons* ■ *The Missionary Under Attack* ■ *Practical Application for Missionaries* ■ *Steps to Freedom in Christ*

Other Good
Harvest House Reading

THE BONDAGE BREAKER YOUTH EDITION
by *Neil Anderson* and *Dave Park*

Do you feel like everybody is a better Christian than you? Is every day a struggle? Pressure from your friends, sexual temptation, insecurity, doubt, and fear can keep you from being the Christian you want to be. And every day you promise God you'll do better—only you don't. *The Bondage Breaker Youth Edition* will help you break free of even the most dangerous habits and private sins. God is not shocked at what you do...He wants to help! Anderson and Park share practical and effective ways to fight Satan's plans to ruin your Christian life. You *can* experience the freedom God wants you to have in your everyday life. Things can be different!

THE BONDAGE BREAKER YOUTH EDITION STUDY GUIDE
by *Neil Anderson* and *Dave Park*

This companion study guide to *The Bondage Breaker Youth Edition* provides *real* answers and *proven* applications to the hard questions you struggle with. This guide will help you learn to recognize where you are in bondage; identify the powerful truths of God's Word; live out these truths in your daily life; and know Christ better and find freedom in Him.

CLASS OF 2000
by *Ginny Williams*

Second Chances. When her widowed father remarries, Kelly vows to never accept his new wife. Then the opportunity comes to work with horses at a summer camp, and Kelly jumps at the chance. Getting away for a couple of months seems to be the perfect solution. But how much longer can Kelly run away from the trouble at home... or the turmoil in her own heart?

A Matter of Trust. Living with a new parent is a lot harder than Kelly thought it would be. Tensions build when Kelly's dad goes on a business trip, leaving Peggy in charge. Kelly constantly finds herself saying and doing things she later regrets. Kelly likes her stepmom—she really does. So why is she having such a hard time getting along with her?

Lost-and-Found Friend. Brent has a lot going for him—good grades, athletic talent, a great girlfriend. But home is a different matter. Greg wants to help his friend, but Brent keeps putting him off. And lately Brent's moodiness and brooding slience have only been getting worse. Will Greg get through to Brent before he tries something desperate?

A Change of Heart. Julie had always thought her faith was strong—but lately she's been having doubts. Surprised and confused by her thoughts, she searches for answers in new friends and a new attitude. If God isn't real, she figures, does it matter how she acts? But how long can Julie avoid the pain in her heart? How long can she keep running from God?

Spring Fever. Everything had been going along fine for Greg and Kelly—until Robbie. There's something about him that Kelly can't resist. Unable to give up Greg, yet curious about the new guy, Kelly tries to have it all. But if Kelly cares so much for Greg, why is she willing to risk everything on a guy she hardly knows?